SILVER
LINING

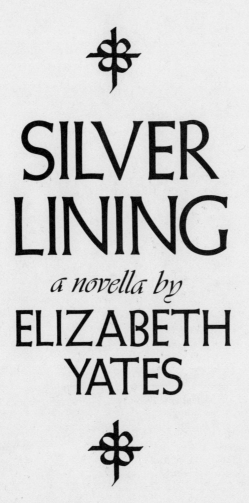

SILVER LINING

a novella by

ELIZABETH YATES

PHOENIX PUBLISHING
Canaan, New Hampshire

Yates, Elizabeth, 1905-
    Silver lining.

    I.   Title
PS3547.A745S5   813'.52   81-15392
ISBN 0-914016-81-4   AACR2
ISBN 0-914016-82-2 (pbk.)

Printed in the United States of America

To
the Martins of this world
whose gift is one
of listening.

Contents

At Rise of Curtain

WHEN THE PEOPLE in
this story walked across
the threshold of my
imagination, they were like actors on a stage. I had not
known them, with perhaps one exception. Bart I knew well,
for he has influenced my life. And the dog was familiar
to me.

They came into my ken as they came into Bart's house,
seeking shelter from a freak snowstorm. I know that kind
of storm: winter coming before the countryside is ready
for it, beauty and ravage in its wake and much of it erased
by the sunshine of a new day. I did not know, at first, that
the people were fleeing anything but the weather. Martin
did. He saw in their eyes what they had neither words nor
willingness to reveal. When I began to see them as he did, I
saw the anguish, the fear, the unresolved turmoil they had
as much need to shed as they did their wet clothes. Given a
climate as warm as it was peaceable, this began to happen
as they talked together. Release came in different ways as the
hours of the stormy night ticked slowly by and the group of
unrelated people became for a brief period a closeknit
family, sharing and caring.

Growing to know them and understand them, affection deepened within me and their words found a way through my pencil almost as if it were dictation I was taking. Each morning, when I went to my desk, I found myself wondering what they would be talking about.

This is a short book, how could it be otherwise? The hours were not long between late afternoon and early morning and some were spent in sleep. Perhaps, now, it is up to you, the reader, to carry on with the more that might be said— either by going back into their lives to find the reasons for their actions or by going forward and imagining what each one will do with the gift of time.

Sydney Cox in *Indirections,* that small but powerful book on writing, says that the end of a story should leave the reader with an upward impulse and a kind of peace. I can leave these people who came across my threshold so unannounced and yet with such urgency because I feel all right about them, whatever may be ahead for them in the bright light of a new day. Do you?

E.Y.

SILVER
LINING

5:OO P.M.

W HAT'S IT MEAN?"
"Those clouds? That
color?"
"Yes."

"Good day tomorrow, but I wouldn't want to say what may happen before morning."

The two men stood on the porch of a small house. One was tall with the lean hard-muscled build of a man whose time was spent largely outdoors. The other was shorter and more compact. He had the look of one who knew how to listen, and he smiled easily. Both had white hair. The taller man's was a thick shock; the other's was thin, but like a coronet it was heaviest around and back of his ears.

They were watching the sun disappear, not behind the distant line of hills, but into a maze of clouds, red, gold, saffron. They were the colors that had recently been on the trees, but the trees were bare now except for an oak that towered near the house. Heavy green foliage, turning slowly to maroon, still clung to its branches and limbs."

"Better plan to spend the night under my roof, Martin,"

1

the taller man said. "I can fix you up all right. There's rain in those clouds, and it could overtake you before you get back to town."

"I'll not question your knowledge of the weather, Bart, and I can't think of anything better than to spend some time with you. Can we get a message to my housekeeper?"

"Ruel will be along soon. He'll make a phone call for you."

"It's so quiet," Martin said approvingly.

"It's not always so." Bart turned his head to listen for sounds on the main road a quarter mile away. The near hills that cupped the house in their embrace acted as a sounding board; but now, at a time of day when traffic was usually heavy, there was none to be heard. Bart liked the rumble and roar of traffic, especially in the late afternoon. It meant people, coming and going, and since he had been alone he liked the thought of people whatever they were doing.

There was more in the west than the spectacular color that attended the sun's disappearing. A wild rack of clouds was bearing down fast, like an army with black banners.

"Rain's on the way," Bart added. "Perhaps rain with a trace of snow, but good weather tomorrow."

"You're going by the old saw 'Red sky at night, shepherd's delight'?"

"Never known it to fail, for shepherd, sailor, farmer, or whoever depends on the weather."

Bart reached down to rest his hand on the head of the dog who stood between them. The collie's tail wagged slowly. Bart felt the dog tense himself. Ears went up, then lowered, and the tail moved faster than ever. There were footsteps on the trail that came down through the woods and went past the house.

"That'll be Ruel." Bart stepped away from the porch, followed by Martin.

Silver Lining

Ruel Gibbs saw them and lifted his hand in greeting. "Good to see you here, Pastor. Been making your calls on foot, as usual?"

"Yes, I have. It gives me time to keep my thoughts in order. We've been watching a mighty handsome show in the west."

"And probably wondering what it means." Ruel manned the fire tower on the summit of Equity, not a mountain but the highest point in the county and one that commanded a wide view of timberland. Firewatching was for dry periods; on rainy days and in the winter Ruel worked as a forester. Radio communication with the tower brought him weather news before it came over the local station.

"What's the latest?" Bart asked.

"Rain, heavy at times. Snow in the higher elevations, that's us. And a twenty-degree drop in temperature, that's us, too."

"Sounds like winter on the way."

"Right. They've closed the road through the pass."

"So that's why I haven't been hearing any traffic."

"Better for people to go forty miles than get stranded on Route 74. Remember that pileup last year when one of the early storms hit? No one wants to go through that again."

"I remember." That was the week Amy died, and Bart was not apt to forget anything that happened during it.

"Since you're on foot, Pastor, I shouldn't advise you trying to make it to town. Lucy would be pleased to have you stay with us."

"Thanks, Ruel, but I've just told Bart I'd stay the night with him, that is, if you'll get a message to my housekeeper to tell her where I am."

"Will do, and she'll know if you're with Bart you'll be all right no matter what the weather does." He turned to Bart. "You set for a couple of days in case we get snowed in?"

Bart smiled as if he was looking forward to such a pros-

5:00 P.M.

pect. "All set for a couple of weeks. Jock and I have sat out more than one storm."

Ruel glanced toward the porch. Hanging on the back wall was some of Bart's equipment—shovel, snowshoes. "You've got what you need to dig yourself out and get down to Lucy and me if need be."

"I like to keep things handy."

Ruel looked at the two men quizzically, tenderly, then smiled. "I'd best be going. Lucy gets a little nervous when weather is threatening. She's alone so much of the time." He raised his right hand. "Take care, you two." Turning, he was off, loping down the trail toward Hemphill.

Martin nudged Bart. "What do you bet he's saying to himself, 'Two old men, they'll sleep the night away and not even know there was a storm.'"

Bart feigned surprise. "Why, Pastor Martin, I didn't think you were a betting man!"

Martin chuckled. "Only when I know I'll win."

"Ready to go inside?"

Martin shook his head. "Not while there's still color in the sky. Think I'll saunter up the trail a bit. It's a treat for me, Bart, to have all this silence. Why, not even the trees are talking!"

"I expect you don't get much quiet in your busy life."

"Only that I make for myself. But here, it's all made for me. I can't afford to pass it up."

"Take Jock along with you. He'll know when you've both gone far enough and will turn you back."

Bart watched Martin move slowly, carefully up the trail, so different from the way Ruel had come down it, but there was more than half a century of years between them. He thought of Lucy waiting to welcome Ruel, the house warm, the good smell of dinner coming from the kitchen. "Alone so much of the time," Bart murmured, hearing again the tenderness in Ruel's words, "and I'm alone all the time."

Silver Lining

He sat down on the porch step and looked off to the west. It was the time of day he and Amy used to keep for themselves, the time when work was over and chores were done, a little hiatus between what the day had been and what the evening might be. Sometimes they talked, sometimes they were silent. If a letter had come from either one of their children, there was always plenty to talk about; but the silence between them was never empty.

It was a different quiet now: no intermittent words, no pressure of a hand, but memories. There had been sorrow during their years, but far more joy, and always a sense of wholeness. That was life, its rhythm, its reality, and those who expected life to be any different were the unprepared. Through easy tenor or occasional distress, Amy never lost her confidence in goodness, and nothing took from her a sense of wonder that appeared to be newly born each day.

Shifting his gaze from the distant hills, Bart could just see the outline of the big house beside the main road. It had been their home for many years when he had farmed the near acres, kept a small herd of cows and a large flock of hens. With a vegetable garden, berry bushes, and fruit trees, they had all worked hard and thrived. Happiness had never been beyond the horizon or at the foot of the rainbow, but at home.

Years pass and ways change. Small farming became impracticable, and the land, in any case, was more suited for timber growing. Bart sold the big house as a summer place for a family from the city and built a small house up on the slope of Equity. It was big enough for himself and Amy, with a tent for the children when they came to visit during the summer; children, now with children of their own. He and Amy had always been proud of them; would always be, he corrected himself.

They had spent forty years of living in the big house, but they had parted with it without regret. Amy had said that giving up things that no longer served a need helped one

5:00 P.M.

5

to give up life when the time came. Often, and clearly, he remembered what she had said: it kept her near. Freed of responsibility, they could still enjoy the big house, keeping an eye on it for the owners when they returned to the city in the fall and harvesting the late fruit, especially the seckel pears that were never ready until after frost.

Sitting in the stillness, with the main road so empty of traffic, Bart felt it was like the way it used to be long ago when the only sound after dark was the clopping of hooves and the frail light flickering on the doctor's buggy as he went up the pass to answer some call that had come down to him.

A sudden gust of wind swept down Equity and rattled the leaves on the oak tree. The sting of cold rain was in the air. Bart heard footsteps, then Martin's voice as he talked to the dog. Soon they were both standing beside him.

"Back just ahead of the rain." Bart clapped his hand on Martin's shoulder.

"Those scudding clouds took the glow from the sky. I was glad to have your dog with me. Night's coming down fast."

"We'll soon have a glow in the house." Bart got up stiffly and gestured toward the door as Martin stepped up to the porch. Then Bart leaned close to Jock. "You go on now, old fellow, and take care of yourself. It may be we won't be opening any doors once this storm gets going."

Obediently but slowly, Jock walked away and toward the woods in a ritual long established.

Even with all he had been seeing, Bart never could resist taking one last look down the hillside sprawling with juniper, across the valley to the distant hills, then up into the oak that loomed near the house. Still heavy with leaves when most of the other trees had shed theirs, he hoped the weather prediction would hold to rain. Snow could put a weight on the leaves that might be more than some limbs

Silver Lining

could handle, especially the big one very close to the house.

"What's on your mind?" Martin was holding the door open.

"The oak. I'm wishing I'd trimmed that leaning limb last summer after a wind wrestled with it and weakened it. Tomorrow I'll ask Ruel to take care of it."

"It must be handy to have a forester for a neighbor when you live on the edge of the woods."

"It is. He's helped me out more than once. But, come on, let's get inside and stir up some warmth."

They went into the house just as the clock chimed the half hour.

"Make yourself at home while I tend to a few things."

"I'll do that," Martin replied.

He knew the house well, for he was a frequent visitor, not only on parish matters, but often for conviviality, and once for comfort. Bart had been more ready than most to meet the loss of the one with whom he had shared life for many years, but just to sit with him by the stove in wordless communication had tided them both over a difficult time. Martin had known Amy as long as he had known Bart, and that was from the time twelve years ago when he had come as pastor to the church in Hemphill. Amy had brought something to him which he had gone without since he had lost his Maria after only five years of marriage.

Martin took off his coat and hung it on the rack near the door. His gaze went around the room with the pleasure gained from familiarity. It was not a large room, but it was adequate, and everything needed to make it comfortable was there—three chairs and one of them a rocker, a table that could be extended when necessary, a shelf of books. An iron stove that served for warmth as well as cooking stood on a hearth of tiles. The rug was worn; the rainbow-

5:00 P.M.

striped curtains at the windows were faded. A bedroom with a small bathroom led off at one side. Near the stove was a door that opened into a pantry, and beyond it was a woodshed.

Bart switched on a light and the room came alive. He opened the door of the stove and stirred the coals, then took a chunk of wood from the box by the stove and put it on the coals. He waited for it to catch and the bark to flame, then closed the door and held his hands to the warmth.

"Pull up the rocker, Martin, and get some of this warmth into you."

Martin did, knowing there was nothing he could do to help Bart. He settled back into the chair and let the warmth embrace him. It was good to sit down. He was more tired than he had realized, and the wind had put a chill in to him during those last few minutes outdoors. Bart turned the knob on the radio but soon turned it off, as it was not time for the news. He brought a kerosene lamp in from the shed and placed it on the table, then went to the door to open it for Jock.

The dog was standing there, wagging his tail in anticipation and whimpering softly. His coat caught in the light was silvery with rain.

Bart heard the rain on the oak leaves, not hard yet but constant. His attention quickened at another sound, almost like the clopping of hooves; almost but not quite. It was not heavy enough, not steady enough. He opened the door wider for the light to flow further. A person was coming up the road. He could see the figure even against the darkness. He waited.

"Hello there," he called when the distance had shortened enough for a voice to be heard. "Hello-o-o."

There was a pause, a halt of the footsteps, and then a voice.

"I saw the light and thought there must be someone

home." It was a woman's voice, slightly out of breath and questioning.

The footsteps resumed, and as they came nearer and into the path of light Bart got a better view. Tweed slacks and a leather jacket said something about the one seeking shelter. Short grayish hair glistened with rain as Jock's coat had. She was carrying a small suitcase.

Bart looked at her shrewdly. Give or take a year or two, she was his age. He smiled in welcome as she stepped onto the porch. He liked the spirit of adventure wherever found or whatever the guise. "Won't you come in?"

He held out his hand. Instead of grasping it, she gave him the suitcase. "I guess you'll have to take me in." Once inside, she shook herself out of her leather jacket and handed it to Bart. "I hardly expected such service, but I certainly need a roof over my head on a night like this. Thank you."

Bart gestured to the facilities off the bedroom, but she would have none of them. "Not yet," she said abruptly.

Then she saw Pastor Martin, standing now with his back to the stove and smiling broadly. He took a step toward her and held out his hand. "I've warmed the rocker for you."

"And I'll soon warm us all with some tea." Bart moved the kettle to the hottest part of the stove and went to the cupboard to get what was needed.

"How lucky can one be!" the newcomer exclaimed as she sank down in the rocker.

"Perhaps we're the lucky ones," Martin said.

Soon all three were sitting close to the stove, warming their hands around mugs of tea, and sipping slowly while the visitor told her story.

"I was on my way out of Hemphill when a state trooper waved me down to a stop. Oh, he was very nice, they always are, and he told me they'd had orders to stop all cars

5:00 P.M.

going through the pass beginning at five o'clock. I looked at my watch and told him it was five minutes to five and that I'd be through the pass in less than fifteen minutes. So he let me go!"

"Gallant fellow," Bart murmured.

"I suspect your watch was a bit slow." Martin smiled slyly.

She answered with a wry smile of her own. "Of course it was. But, wouldn't you know, I was just giving my car the gas for the long pull uphill when the engine sputtered and moaned. You can guess what that meant! I managed to coast into the driveway of the first house I saw to ask for help, but I soon discovered that there was no one home. The house was closed. It seemed a good enough place to spend the night in the car, and I was getting ready to do just that when I saw your light come on."

"We're glad to have your company, Mrs. ———"

"Thurston. Mrs. Dexter Thurston. Helen."

Bart inclined his head slightly. "Bartholomew Wilmer, Bart. This is Pastor Martin Amblin. My dog's name is Jock."

At sound of his name, Jock looked up from licking his paws but, seeing that nothing was expected of him, returned to his licking.

Helen's eyes swept the room. Her glance took in the small bedroom and the half-open door near the stove. She turned to Bart. "Can you put me up for the night? I'll gladly sleep on the floor. Or—" she hesitated "—I could go back to my car."

"Of course I can put you up, and comfortably. The bedroom will be yours. Martin and I will do quite well in this room."

"And we'll keep each other awake as we keep the fire alive."

Helen had no reason to doubt their sincerity, but something about the situation suddenly struck her as funny. She put back her head and laughed. "Done in by an act of God when the law would have saved her! Sounds like a juicy headline or a lead for a scenario."

"I don't like attributing the weather, or any unusual occurrence, to God." Bart shook his head in disapproval.

"Oh, you don't? Well, what shall we say when something unexpected and quite out of one's control happens?"

Bart shrugged. "Happenstance."

Helen again gazed around the room. Simple and neat as it was, a woman's touch was evident: the pretty cloth on the table, the plants near one of the windows. "Your wife?" she asked tentatively.

"Amy exchanged this world for another a year ago, about this time."

Helen started to speak, then stopped. Sympathy scarcely seemed in order when Bart's attitude implied that death had come as naturally as the going down of the sun at the end of a satisfying day. She waited a decent interval, then said, "Another world. You really believe that, Bart?"

"Yes, with my heart and with my mind. I haven't the slightest idea what it will be like, except that it will be different from this."

"Amy always wondered what was beyond the horizon," Martin put in gently, "not of the hills she could see but of the ones the eye cannot see. Now she knows."

Helen looked at him as if she would expect that kind of remark from a pastor, but it was not the time for argument so she turned back to Bart. "And you will find each other again?"

"Yes."

"Physical resemblance?"

"I doubt it."

"But how will you know each other?"

Bart went back in memory to the time when he and Amy

5:00 P.M.

had first met. It was at a church picnic. She was carrying a basket, and he had offered to carry it for her. The way she smiled when she said, "Yes, thank you," had gone to his heart. Their eyes met, and he knew then. The more they saw each other, the more they shared thoughts and ideas, the more surely they knew they were meant for each other; but it was two years before they were married.

He was working the land at the base of Equity, making it into a productive farm. She was teaching in the elementary school at Hemphill. He wanted to see a house built, doing much of the work on it himself, before he brought her to it as his wife; she wanted to go on with the teaching for which she had trained. "When you're sure, you can wait," she had said then. She had said the same words often during the years.

Helen nudged herself into his reverie, repeating her question. "Bart, how will you and Amy know each other?"

"How can I say? But I think it will be the way it was when we first met. We knew."

Martin moved his head in affirmation. "Qualities. They drew Maria and me at first; they'll draw us again sometime."

Helen did not hear, so intent was she on Bart. "And you're ready?" There was a tenderness in her tone which had not been evident before.

"Yes, oh yes." Bart said and nodded. He had gone through too much during the last year to say just how ready he felt.

"So am I. I'm always ready."

Bart glanced at the suitcase he had set down by the door and chuckled. "So I see."

"But not to meet Dexter Thurston!" Helen exclaimed with some vehemence. "I had enough of him in this life. I'll be on the lookout for new experiences."

"I'm sure there'll be plenty."

Silver Lining

The small clock on the shelf above the books tinkled six musical notes. The sound was like that of an old-fashioned music box, and the reminder of the hour was of gaiety more than urgency.

"Friendly little clock," Helen commented.

"Yes, it is a friend, and an old one at that. Someone brought it to Amy from Switzerland a good many years ago." Bart, standing up, went over to the radio. "Time for the news." He turned it on at the moment that a thumping sounded on the door. Turning it off, he went to the door and opened it.

A young man stood on the threshold, wet and shivering. The only part of him that was dry was his hair when he pulled his helmet off. A golden-headed boy, Bart thought, as he held out his hand in welcome.

"I saw your light, thought perhaps you could tell me how near I am to a garage."

"You're not far, two miles or so down the road, but you'll not find one open at this hour and on a night like this. Come on in."

"But my motorbike has blown a tire. I've got to get it fixed so I can be on my way."

"Tomorrow will be soon enough. The roads are treacherous now." Bart grasped the young man's hand and drew him into the room. "I'm Bart Wilmer."

"My name's Gabe Smith."

Bart helped Gabe off with his jacket, dripping wet as it was, and hung it on the rack. "You're not the only one to take shelter from the storm. Come near the warmth and join us."

Gabe stared, wondering what he had got himself into; an old folks' home, perhaps. "Thanks, but I really must get on my way." Drawn partly by Bart's hand on his arm, partly by the warmth he desperately needed, Gabe approached the stove. "Well, perhaps just until I get dry." He

5:00 P.M.

saw Helen and held out his hand to her. "Mrs. Wilmer?"

"No, Mrs. Thurston." She took his hand, amused at the slight consternation she had caused him.

Gabe acknowledged Pastor Martin with an inclination of his head. "Oh, am I breaking up some kind of party?"

"Not at all, you're adding to it," Martin said, drawing up another chair.

"I'm on my way to Atherston," Gabe explained. "I blew a tire. Saw a car parked by a big house down the road, so I pulled in beside it. Then I saw the light from this house and came for some information."

Helen leaned toward him. "That's my car down by the house. You and I are in the same fix. Come on up closer to the stove, young man, you're wet."

"Wet is no word for it," Gabe admitted. "It's raining hard. There's ice on the road. Slipping and sliding, I didn't know whether or not I'd make it. But I've got to get on my way."

Bart pressed a mug of tea into Gabe's hands.

Gabe put it to his lips and gulped swiftly, then exclaimed at the heat. "Sorry, guess I took it too fast." He rubbed the back of a hand across his lips.

"Hurry won't do any more good with a cup of tea than it will on any icy road," Bart said. "Now, sit down and make yourself at home. We're all here until morning, or until the storm stops, whichever comes first."

"But I've got to get my tire fixed. I've got to move along. I've—"

"Forget it, Gabe," Bart said, putting a hand on his shoulder and pushing him gently into the chair. "Nothing can happen for any of us until morning. There are times in life when weather is the great arbiter, and this is one of those times."

Helen looked at Gabe with the sympathy she felt Bart

had not needed. "I've got to get on my way, too, Gabe, but neither of us can do it for a few hours." She wanted to say, "Make the best" but changed to, "Why don't you just enjoy this unusual situation which we find ourselves in?"

Gabe sighed and put the mug to his lips gingerly.

"I'm not sure that you all know each other." Bart gestured to one then another. "This is Pastor Martin; my dog's name is Jock. Gabe Smith."

"Short for Gabriel," Martin said approvingly.

"How'd you guess!" There was an edge of bitterness to the tone. "Imagine going through life with a name like that!"

Bart crossed the room to switch on the radio, but before he got to it the lights flickered and went out. The only light in the room came from the cracks in the stove.

"There'll be no news tonight," Helen said.

"Ice on the wires," Bart added as he went to the table where he had placed the kerosene lamp.

"No news," Gabe repeated. "That's good." He settled back into his chair with a look of relief. He sipped his tea. "And this is good."

Bart struck a match and lit the lamp. Its soft glow filled the room, touching everything soothingly. Martin's plump cheeks shone with something more than health. Gabe's golden curls looked like an aureole. A restfulness had settled over Helen. As Bart pulled up a chair to complete the half circle by the stove, it seemed to him as if peace had pervaded the room, peace that was in sharp contrast to the storm that was beginning to make itself felt outside, as the rain turned to snow. He reached down to run his hand over Jock's fur. The dog sighed, aware of contentment that was as real as warmth. The clock announced the half hour in its cheerful way, and Bart realized that he must soon start putting together some supper for

5:00 P.M.

his guests. But he was loath to interrupt the comfortable quiet that had come over them all. A long night was before them. It would not matter when they ate.

The quiet was intruded upon by the sound of footsteps on the porch and a baby's long wail. Jock barked sharply and ran to the door. Gabe looked startled and said, "What's that?" Bart rose from his chair slowly and crossed the room toward the door.

"More guests?" Helen asked. "But there's no more room."

"This house is expandable," Martin said, "you'll see."

"Come in," Bart called as he approached the door.

They came, a girl and a young man, each with long hair hanging lank. He had a heavy packframe on his back; she had a small child riding in a carrier on her shoulders. They were covered with snow.

"Well, well," Bart began, finally making "Welcome" out of his surprise. He took a broom and brushed the snow off them so it could melt on the floor, then eased the carrier from the girl's shoulders. "Give us a hand, Gabe."

Gabe came forward and helped with the packframe. The two new arrivals looked dazed and weary. If they said anything by way of explanation, their words were lost in the child's crying.

Bart took the baby from the carrier. Crossing the room, he placed it on Helen's lap, then took a towel from a stand near the stove and handed it to her.

"I don't know what to do with a baby," Helen protested. "Never had one in my life."

"Do what its mother would do if she were able," Bart said in an authoritative tone. "Warm it, cuddle it."

He returned to the young couple still near the door. The girl had sunk down to the floor; her head was in her hands, and her wet hair hung forward like a curtain.

Silver Lining

"I'm so tired. I couldn't go any longer." She started sobbing into her cupped hands.

She can't be twenty, Bart thought, then reminded himself that the older he got the younger the young seemed to appear.

"Let her rest. She'll be all right in a few minutes," the young man said.

"But you're both soaking wet, and you must be cold. Draw up to the stove." Kindly as Bart's tone was, it carried something approaching command.

Gabe helped them ease out of their jackets, then he draped them over the rack to dry.

The girl struggled to her feet. Pushing her hair away from her face, she looked at Bart, and he saw how pale she was. Tears had washed the color from her eyes. He put his hand under her arm and helped her toward the stove. The young man followed. The two of them sat down on the floor cross-legged and held out their hands to the warmth. Bart gave his name, then nodded toward the others in turn as he introduced them, not forgetting Jock.

"I'm Val," the young man said, "she's Vera." Last name or names were not included in his brief introduction.

"It seems the storm is making us into a family," Martin observed affably. "When you're warmed up a bit and have got some tea inside you, tell us about yourselves."

Their story was soon told, and all by Val. They had been living in a commune for a year, off the land and by their own hands; but one winter had been enough and everyone had begun to disperse. They had decided to head for the Southwest and had been hitchhiking for the past week.

"I'm so tired," Vera whispered.

"She's always tired," Val explained, "born that way. We had a good ride today in a cattle truck as far as Hemphill,

5:00 P.M.

then they rerouted traffic because of the weather. We decided to keep on, figuring we could sleep out the storm somewhere. But—"there was a long pause"—then we saw your light."

"You were going to sleep out in this weather?" Martin asked.

"Oh, sure. We have our sleeping bags."

"With the baby?" Helen was incredulous. Struggling awkwardly with the child, she had finally gotten her wet clothes off and wrapped her in the warm towel. Still awkwardly but with a certain amount of satisfaction, she cozied the baby on her lap.

"It wouldn't be the first time."

"You've gotten her quiet," Vera said more audibly. A smile flickered momentarily as she looked up at Helen.

"What's her name?" Helen asked.

"Baby."

"I take it she's never been baptized," Martin said.

"Often enough by the rain," Val answered for them both, "but even it's polluted now."

Bart had gone into the bedroom and was busying himself there. When he returned, he went up to Val. "I've put some clothes out on the bed in there. Use whatever you fancy, but take off those wet things."

"We're used to wet clothes."

"Not in my house when you can have dry ones. You'll find as much as you need, both of you, and I've got something here for the baby. There's a bathroom through that door."

Val looked ready to speak. Then, as if something had changed his mind, he put his hand on Vera's shoulder. They got to their feet and went into the bedroom, closing the door behind them.

Bart handed some baby garments to Helen. "These'll be dry and warm, but they may be old-fashioned."

Silver Lining

Helen took them eagerly. After first rubbing the baby with the towel, she slipped a little shirt on over its head and found a button to secure it. She wrapped another, smaller towel into a makeshift diaper, then covered it with a pair of pants. Bart, watching her, thought he could have done a better job, but she seemed to be enjoying what she was doing. Gurgles of laughter from the child made a game of the performance.

19

Gabe let out a long low whistle as if he'd been holding his breath. "You're going to civilize them, Bart."

"And I'd like to see that little one have a name before the night's out," Martin said.

"We'll all be wanting something to eat," Bart added. "Think we're likely to have any more visitors?" His glance went to Martin, then to Gabe. "Let's take a look and see what the weather is up to."

The three men, followed by Jock, went out to stand on the porch. It was snowing hard; the fall was as steady and relentless as the rain had been earlier.

"I guess we're in for it," Martin commented.

Bart smiled. Something in him had a relish for rough weather. It was a different world from the one he and Martin had been in when they watched the sunset colors obscured by the race of black clouds. As the wind picked up, bearing rain, there had been a wild beauty to the night with leaves scuttering over the ground and those that had not fallen rattling in the oak that swung by the house. Now the snow imposed quiet. Smoke from the fire in the stove drifting down and around them meant there had been no shift in the wind.

"Is it true that one can hear the snow fall?" Gabe asked.

"Maybe for your young ears, but I doubt if either Bart or I can."

"Poor old motorbike! It must be just about buried by now, along with Mrs. Thurston's car."

5:00 P.M.

"I knew the way those clouds were sagging that they had moisture in them," Bart said, shaking his head.

"What's wrong with a little water?" Gabe asked. "In California it seems we're always needing it. If it isn't for the land, it's to quench brushfires."

"Oh, we need it all right, especially now before the ground freezes, but snow—this heavy wet kind is something different. The weight of it—"Bart stopped short.

Gabe looked puzzled. "You mean we're going to be snowed in?"

Bart nodded.

"Well, if that's the case—" Gabe, followed by Martin, left the porch for the trees. The tracks they made in the snow soon began to fill.

Bart looked at the oak, a great hulk only a little darker than the darkness around him. He had had many conversations with it, more since he had been alone, and the oak had its way of replying—a whispering of leaves, a rubbing together of branches, sometimes a spate of sound when the wind raced through it. Now, under its weight of snow, it was silent and Bart was uneasy. He stepped down from the porch to look more closely up into it. Two strides and he could have put his hands on the fissured bark of its stalwart trunk, but he stayed near the porch. Even in the slim light that came from the house he saw that his hands would not have met the familiar touch of bark, for the oak was coated with a film of ice.

Every leaf, every twig, every branch, and the bole itself was ice encased. What a rattling there'll be when the wind comes along, Bart thought. Wishing the snow might still be rain, he watched it as it fell, layering a little more, a little more on leaves and branches.

He could hear the sound of voices from inside and he could hear Gabe and Martin talking together as they trudged back to the porch; he was aware of the low whining that came from Jock as the dog nuzzled his knee and tried to get his attention. Bart, as encased in silence as the tree was in ice, held his face up, feeling the snow on his brow, on his cheeks, on his lips.

"It's a taste of winter long before it's due," he said as he joined the two who were waiting for him.

"I'd call it a big bite," Martin commented.

"I'm going in. I'm cold." Gabe pushed the door open and went in to the lamplit room.

Martin saw Bart look back at the oak. He caught the small sound of a sigh.

"What is it, Bart?"

"I wanted them to be comfortable, now I hope they'll be safe. They're all edgy about what the weather may do to them. How can I give them some kind of assurance when my concern is with the tree and its weight of snow?"

"It's not the weather, Bart, ominous as it may seem, so much as their own lives. Each one has some private anxiety, except the baby, God bless her. Nervousness about the storm may prove to be a convenient cover-up."

Bart sighed again, but with relief as a weight that had begun to burden him was lifted. Years of living had told him that there was little a man could do about the weather but make the best of it. Martin knew of another kind of weather and knew how to cope with it. He put his hand on Martin's shoulder. "I'll do what I can to keep them warm and fed. The rest is up to you."

"As opportunity offers."

They went toward the door and into the warm room. Jock shook his coat free of snow and followed them.

"Not likely there'll be any more visitors with the way the snow is piling up," Bart made his pronouncement casually.

Baby, awake and being bounced on Helen's knees, beamed at them; then, with a determination that went far

5:00 P.M.

beyond her size, she struggled to the floor and crawled rapidly toward Jock.

Helen smoothed her slacks, oblivious to the dampness on her knees.

"She's always like that when she sees an animal," Val explained.

Jock, realizing that he was soon to be the object of attention, sat down and thumped his tail. Baby snuggled close to him, exploring his long nose and soft ears with her small hands. She ran them over his coat, then pushed him so he would be lying down and there would be a place for her beside him. Jock made inner sounds of pleasure while his tail moved faster.

Bart said, "He's always had parental leanings."

Watching them, Bart felt happy for the dog and the child. Like two long separated friends united, they were quietly enjoying each other's company. He could see both parents in the child. That red mop of hair was her father's, the blue eyes her mother's. Positive identification somehow pleased him. He was glad to know she was theirs, even though they had not apparently made much place for her in their lives. As the child was dressed now in some woolies his own children had worn, he could see she was sturdy with well-formed arms and legs. Bart had seen enough of generation, both animal and human, to appreciate a good body.

"How old is she?"

"About a year," Val said.

Vera answered more precisely, "She's eleven months."

This time, as she looked up at him, Bart saw Vera's eyes clearly. Free from the tears that had clouded them, their blue was heightened by the blue of the dressing gown she had put on. Blue-eyed people should always wear blue clothes, he thought, then reminded himself that she had put on the gown for its warmth and because he had laid it

Silver Lining

out for her. Her brown hair was dry now and hung below her shoulders. Her cheeks had lost their pallor and were beginning to glow from the warmth of the stove. She looked almost pretty, and Bart wondered if she was finding some kind of satisfaction in being a woman again, or looking like one in any case. She was sitting on the floor with her knees drawn up to her chest, and the blue robe was so long that only her bare toes peeped out from under it. Bart hoped that something of Amy's mantle might fall on Vera with the robe, even if just for this one night.

"She's happy," Vera added, as if whatever responsibility she might feel for the child was set aside. "That means she'll be quiet."

"Has she had anything to eat?"

"Yes, Bart," Helen replied quickly. "I found some bread and milk in your pantry, and she seemed satisfied."

"She'll eat anything," the mother said.

"Or what she can get," the father added.

"Food!" Bart exclaimed. "That's what we're all wanting. I'll have a look to see what I can give you."

Only the day before Bart had made a large stew following one of Amy's dictums: "When you make a stew make a big one, for it's always good to have on hand." Ruel had brought him five pounds of beef; there were carrots and onions in plenty from his own garden, and he was never at a loss for potatoes. Looking around his pantry storeroom, he noted apples and cheese, two loaves of Lucy Gibbs' bread, a pound of butter, a whole can of coffee. Milk was not plentiful, and what there was would be saved for Baby. He would set some aside for a morning meal, and by noon he would probably be alone again. If he and Martin and the two young men could not shovel a path down to the road, Ruel would be along to help them. He always did turn up when a storm was over.

"We shall feast like kings," he called back to the others,

5:00 P.M.

"but it will take awhile for the stew to warm through, and I'll need some help with the vegetables."

Helen was the first to appear at the door, and Bart soon put her to work. Then he carried the iron pot of stew to the stove and set it on the hot surface.

"Gabe, keep an eye to the fire now that we need it for cooking as well as warmth. Martin, you've had enough meals in this house to know how to set the table." Bart glanced at the young couple, sitting back to back on the floor and close to the stove, and added, "I'll put you to work later."

Vera's smile was all the reply he needed.

Perched on a stool by the counter, Helen started to prepare the vegetables. Working neatly and efficiently, she cut carrots and potatoes into small pieces so once the stew started bubbling they could go in with the meat and onions and not take long to cook. Bart assembled knives, forks, plates, and napkins on a tray and handed it to Martin. Then he took a clean cloth and busied himself polishing apples. When Martin had finished setting the table, he joined Bart and Helen in the pantry.

"I'm sure I've seen that young fellow, Gabe, before," Martin said as he pulled a stool up to the counter and sat beside Helen.

"If you live long enough," Bart said, chuckling, "you'll feel that way about everyone."

Talk from the three together by the stove drifted toward the pantry.

"They're getting to know each other," Helen said.

"The way they're going you'd think they'd always known each other."

"Listen!" Martin cocked his head, then put a finger to his lips. "They're talking about us."

"Us?" Helen's eyebrows went up.

Martin tapped his lips with the finger, making a plea for silence.

"You old eavesdropper," Bart whispered.

"What people say in normal voices can be heard by people with normal ears," Martin replied softly.

"Right." Helen kept volume out of her tone and put energy into her cutting.

The three in the pantry listened while words from the three by the stove filtered back to them. Gabe was the most easily articulate, and his voice had a carrying quality. It seemed near at times, then more distant.

"Take it easy, Gabe. You're like an animal in a cage pacing around like that."

"Sometimes I feel just like an animal in a cage."

"Forget it, for tonight anyway. The old fellow is mighty decent to put us all up like this."

"You don't suppose they can hear us, do you?"

"Of course not! Old people are always hard of hearing."

"And not particularly interested in people like us."

"Right."

"It must be awful to get old."

"Why?" The voice demanding an answer came from the far end of the room. "Why, any more so than to get born? It all seems irrational to me."

"To feel useless, not to be able to do anything."

"The old fellow must get through quite a lot of work. Wonder how he does it."

"Probably has someone to help him."

"You think he's older than the pastor?"

"Could be, but the woman's the oldest."

"What makes you think that? They've all got white hair."

"Her skin is so wrinkled."

Gabe's voice cut through the drone of the two V's,

5:00 P.M.

" 'Thus is her cheek the map of days outworn.' "

"Well said."

"Not by me, by Will Shakespeare. It's a line from *The Sonnets* that always stood out to me in freshman English."

"Why ever that one?"

"Why ever not? I suppose it fascinated me because I have no intention of getting old."

There was a snort of laughter from Val. "Better die young, then."

"I plan to."

"So, you've worked out your life to that fine point?"

In the pantry, Martin's lips moved. "I want to hear this. It may help me to understand some attitudes of the young." He leaned his head toward the open door.

"We all thought that way once," Bart murmured.

"They're talking like this because they think there's no future for them," Helen reminded them.

Martin motioned for silence.

"Come on, Gabe, tell us how you're going to manage all this so neatly." Vera's tone was persuasive.

"Yes, I'd like to know." Val's was envious.

"It's quite simple. To begin with, I come of healthy stock and I was brought up to live right—good diet, think positively, exercise, all that. I believe that life is to be enjoyed, and when I can no longer enjoy it I'll opt for out."

"When will that be?"

"Oh, somewhere in my late forties or early fifties, with the first gray hairs, the first twinge of stiffening joints. Why clutter up the earth with another old man?"

"I hope he isn't forgetting to watch the stew," Bart whispered.

Helen pointed to the bowl of vegetables ready to go into it.

"Give them another minute," Martin pleaded. "We're

really getting somewhere."

"—still don't see how you're going to manage your exit."

"Oh, I'll manage. Same way I have everything else up to now."

"You make it all sound so easy."

"Of course it's easy! Life is a problem to be solved, and that's my way of solving it."

"Then the animal will be out of the cage."

"Exactly!"

"I'm hungry." Vera's tone rose as if she wanted to be overheard.

Gabe laughed. "Isn't that just like a woman! In a deep philosophical discussion she suddenly thinks of her stomach! You won't have to wait much longer, Vera, the stew's beginning to bubble. Bart," Gabe called, "are the vegetables ready?"

Helen took the bowl into the other room and tipped its contents into the stew in the iron pot. "Another few minutes and we'll be feasting." She crossed the room to see how Baby was faring. Curled up against the dog, the child was fast asleep. Jock did not so much as raise his head. One eye opened and closed again; the tail lifted and then went limp.

Reaching down to stroke him Helen said, "You know what that child needs most of all, a haven of warmth and comfort, and you're giving it to her."

The tail moved again. An eyelid flickered.

Gabe went to a window to observe the weather. "Snow's still falling, flakes seem heavier. Looks as if we may have to dig ourselves out come morning."

Helen stood beside him, glad she was not in her car. "Falling so straight, so steadily, as if it were never going to stop."

5:00 P.M.

"Maybe we'll all be buried alive."

"Like the thought?" Helen caught herself from saying more.

Gabe stared at her, wondering how much of their conversation might have drifted out to the pantry.

Helen slipped her arm through his. "We're going to enjoy tonight, remember? Let's let tomorrow take care of itself."

It was not long before Bart announced that the stew was on the table. Standing by his chair and gesturing to Martin to sit opposite him, he indicated to Gabe and Helen their places on one side, the two V's on the other. The lamp in the center of the table glowed on the food, making it look as palatable as it smelled. It lit up the glasses that Bart had filled from the gallon jug that was on a small table nearby.

"Water from the spring high on Equity," Bart said, "crystal-clear and cold, probably the purest water some of you wayfarers have had in a long time."

They stood by their chairs, waiting for a signal from their host. Bart gave it as he lifted his glass and held it toward the light. Looking across the table, he raised his eyebrows slightly. "Will you, Martin?"

"With pleasure." Martin closed his eyes for a moment and said a few heartfelt words of blessing. When he opened them he held his glass high. "To the *future!*"

"What's that?" Val muttered.

Martin touched his lips to the glass and smiled at his old friend across the table. Their eyes met. Then Martin held his glass toward each one in turn and sat down. The religious life had schooled him to be expectant of good, and it was clear that a good meal was his immediate future.

"I never knew water could taste like this," Val said.

"It's almost like wine." There was amazement in Vera's voice.

"Better," Helen said.

"Better for you," Gabe added.

The Swiss clock tinkled seven notes, but they went unheard as chairs were drawn out and drawn in again. Soon
the clink of cutlery on plates, the circling of conversation
filled the room; and there were moments of silence that
meant as much as any words to Bart as his guests occupied
themselves with their eating.

5:00 P.M.

7:00 P.M.

T HAT was a very special stew," Gabe said after a second helping had gone around and the iron pot was empty.

"I've tried to remember Amy's way of doing things," Bart replied, "and a stew was one of her favorites." Talking about her seemed to make her one of the group at the table, and it seemed right. So often they had sat with friends around that table and, as often, talked long after the meal was finished. "She was a great one for using everything that came to hand. Finding it or raising it, she could always put it to some good purpose, and a little of this with a little of that went into the making of a stew."

"As frugal a woman as she was prudent," Martin added. "Once I got to know her, I felt that everything I learned of real value came from her."

"She used to say that about you, Martin."

"Did she, now?" There was delight in Martin's smile.

"Amy took life as it came to her, growing older as we all do—" Bart glanced around the table "—but she seemed to

30

be able to meet the changes imposed without resistance."

Val looked skeptical.

"Was she pretty?" Vera asked.

Bart looked at Martin to answer the question.

The pastor's eyes had been half closed, the better to recall the person they were talking about. "Pretty is as pretty does," he said softly.

"Yes, but—" Vera obviously had a gauge to measure people against.

"If you saw her in a crowd you would not have noticed her particularly—medium height, brown hair until it grayed, eyes of no certain color."

"They were blue, Martin."

"So they were." Martin went on as if he had not been interrupted. "But, in that crowd, if you had lost something, or lost your way, or been caught in a turn of events with which you could not cope, she would have been the one most ready to give some kind of help. You would have been aware of her eyes then, not so much their color as their compassion, and you would not have forgotten her."

"I get you." Vera was satisfied.

"And you said she died about a year ago."

"Yes, Helen, almost to the day."

"What—" Helen stopped abruptly. That was not a question to ask.

Bart opened his hands and held them out before them all, studying them for a moment. "Why shouldn't you know what happened? Time happened, as it does for us all. It was a usual day, except that it was the day of the week when she did her baking. That bread lasted me for a month. She made jam, too, as some late pears had ripened, and she never could let anything go to waste if she could help it.

"We sat on the porch and watched the sun go down behind the hills. Now and then she put her hand on her chest where, I knew, there had been recurrent pain. I asked her if I should not get the doctor, but she did not want me to. 'I'm tired, Bart,' she said. 'I'll just go in and rest awhile.' The way she said it, and the way she looked at me, told more than any further words."

"Oh, but," Vera exclaimed impulsively, "shouldn't you have done something? Couldn't you—"

Bart gazed at her tenderly, the girl who was always tired thinking of the woman whose tiredness was of another kind. He smiled, shaking his head slowly. "There's a pear tree down by the big house whose fruit loosens its hold with ripeness. Amy was like that. Her hand had always been so firm on life, but when it came time she let go as easily as fruit dropping."

"*Ripeness.*" Helen said the word as if it was new to her vocabulary.

"Her apprenticeship was over," Martin said.

"Whatever do you mean by that?" Val asked.

"I think the Master Craftsman had other work for her and that she was ready to do it."

There was silence around the table. Bart refilled the glasses. They sipped and savored.

Vera was the first to speak. "Almost you make me want to go on living, to find out some of the things she found out. Almost."

"It's living that does it." Martin looked at Vera as if they were the only two at the table. "Education may prepare one, books will guide one, friends can help one, but it's just plain ordinary daily life that does it."

"I've had a couple of years of philosophy in my college courses, but it never gave me anything like this."

Gabe's comment brought Bart out of the reverie he had slipped into. "Amy's philosophy was a simple one. There was nothing profound about it."

Silver Lining

"Can you put it into words?"

"Oh, into a sentence," Bart replied quickly. "It was to do everything for God and not to mind that some of the things were so little."

"And another point—" Martin raised a finger for attention "—she was convinced that whatever happened she was always in God's care."

"Might be all right for her, living where she did and as she did, but for most of us highly questionable." There was cynicism in Val's voice.

"Yes, of course, because everything is subject to question." Martin found it easier to agree with the young man who was so obviously out of sympathy with the trend of the conversation; but his agreement was only temporary. Before the evening was over, he would challenge Val's point of view.

"Amy always seemed to have an authority to back her up." Bart reached into an inner pocket and drew out a piece of paper which he unfolded carefully. "She must have known what was coming, for she left a note for me. I found it the next day in the drawer with my socks." His eyes rested lovingly on the paper.

Looking at Amy's handwriting was like looking at her picture—the quiet decisiveness, the sure generosity, the spacing, the rhythm. Bart read the words aloud; he could have said them without reading he knew them so well: " 'To those persons who put themselves completely in God's hands, and seek with all diligence to do his will, all that God gives is best of all.' "

"Meister Eckhart," Martin added.

"Yes." Bart folded the paper and returned it to his pocket. "One of her mentors."

Val shook his head, but the motion went unobserved, as all eyes were on Bart.

7:00 P.M.

"You two seemed to have everything." Gabe's tone was close to being reverential. "Yet you've lived in this out-of-the-way place, miles from any city."

"Hemphill is only two miles away, and it's quite a town." Martin was quick in defense of their community.

Gabe moved his hand, gesturing to include himself and the two V's. "Look at us! We've had the world, or as much as we've wanted of it, and it hasn't given us happiness. Or has it?" He looked at Val, then at Vera, and less certainly at Helen sitting beside him.

"Oh," she said, "I suppose I've been happy enough at times. In my way."

"We haven't any roots, that's our trouble." Val broke his dissident silence. "When you don't have roots, you don't seem to have goals."

"You have Baby," Helen reminded him.

Val brushed away the remark as if he were brushing away a fly.

"Give yourselves time, Val," Bart said. "It takes time."

"Time?" Val scoffed. "What is it?"

"Raw material with which to work, no more, no less."

"It must be awful to be without Amy." Vera spoke as if she had not heard the recent conversation. "Awful." She could understand a void; there had been so many in her life.

"Yes, it is," Bart replied gently, "and yet, no. Her thinking is still with me, and I can't help but feel that the way she went was an answer to her prayer for a good death."

"Good for her, perhaps, but not for you."

Bart smiled. There was much he could say, but there was a limit to what others could hear. "It won't be long before we pick up the threads again."

"You really believe that?" Val's tone was incredulous.

"I have no doubt."

"According to your faith be it unto you," Martin said,

"and that, my friends, is a proper ending to our meal."

"Yes." Bart pushed his chair back and stood up. "Let's move toward the stove with those apples I polished for you."

There was a general shift of positions. Helen and Vera took the dishes to the pantry and commenced the washing up. Bart added more wood to the stove. Gabe walked to the window to see what the weather was doing and, while there, Bart called to him to set the jug of water on the porch so it would keep cool. Gabe did so, and when he returned to the others standing near the stove his comment was a laconic "Still snowing."

"But not blowing?"

"Doesn't seem to be."

Bart wondered if he should say anything about the oak and the weight building up on its limbs. He decided not to. No need to introduce anxiety into a group that was finding its way into cordial relationship. Morning would be soon enough to assess their situation, dig themselves out, and get down to the road; or perhaps the road would get up to them if the town crews got an early start with their plowing.

"Nothing like having some good food inside you," Martin said as he settled into one of the chairs drawn up to the stove.

"How about an apple?" Bart passed the bowl around. "These few are the first from a tree I set out last spring. It will bear more next year."

"But they're special, and you're going to give them all to us?" Val was as unbelieving of the offer as he was of the afterlife.

"Tonight is special. There just may not be another one like it in all our lives."

Helen and Vera soon came back from the pantry, their work done. Both looked relaxed and at ease. Vera's smile

7:00 P.M.

had been uncertain at first; now it lighted her face frequently.

"Nothing like doing dishes together to get acquainted," Helen said as she sat in the rocker and sighed contentedly.

Vera sat on the floor near Val, using him as a backrest. Gabe sprawled flat, his head near the group, the rest of him stretched out with feet toward the door. Bart and Martin sat on either side of Helen. Turning her head from time to time, Helen kept an eye on the baby, but there seemed little chance of her waking until some inner urgency occurred.

Seeing the glances cast by Helen across the room, Vera said, "She's a good sleeper—at night, that is. Always has been. As long as the dog doesn't move, she probably won't make a sound until morning. But then—"

"Then she'll be ready to go," Val sighed, "and long before any of us are ready to wake up."

"I'll take care of her, and you two can sleep all morning," Helen said, smiling indulgently. "How's that?"

"Just what the doctor ordered." Val slumped lower and Vera slumped with him.

Gabe's words were drowsy. "It wouldn't take much to put me to sleep, but I'd rather go on talking if anyone else is so inclined." He waited for someone to pick up his invitation. Since no one did, he made a semblance of sleep.

"What's your destination, Gabe?"

Gabe opened his eyes and looked at Martin. "Heaven, I might say, and thereby quote a famous novelist."

"The ultimate, of course, for all of us, but how about the immediate?"

Gabe pulled up his legs and himself into a sitting position so he could face the pastor. "I don't want to go too far back, so let me say that when my college career was summarily

Silver Lining

terminated I decided to see the world on *Bucephalus,* my motorbike."

Martin studied the young face, so close to him that he could have laid his hand on the curly hair. "I've seen you somewhere, Gabe."

"Not possible, sir. I've never been in this part of the country."

Bart looked at the two, one as eager to find a relationship as the other was to avoid it. Summarily terminated, Bart repeated to himself, thinking that the words were almost too carefully chosen.

"You won't believe me, but then you don't have to," Helen said. She took over the conversation and continued it with a lively description of her many travels and the people she had met. She interspersed it with occasional exclamations of relief that she was not spending the night in the cramped and frigid discomfort of a snow-covered car. "Two weeks from now I'll be on my way to Fiji. One of those tours, you know, with people you've never seen before and may never see again. But that's like tonight, isn't it? Fiji is one place I've never been to. Then—" she stopped short. She had no intention of telling anyone what she had been told at the clinic that morning.

"And then?" Vera prompted.

"That's it."

"Oh."

For a few moments there seemed nothing more to be said by anyone.

"Travel's a great way to take up your time," Helen added as an afterthought. "Bart, why don't you get around and see the world before it's too late?"

Bart shook his head. "My sights are set for another shore."

The clock played out its merry tune, marking the passage of another hour.

7:00 P.M.

8:00 P.M.

"I HAVEN'T BEEN so comfortable in a long time," Gabe said, and his words made him spokesman for them all.

"I don't want tonight ever to end," Vera murmured, reaching for Val's hand and impulsively bringing it to her lips. She turned so she could put her head in his lap. "I'm sleepy."

"We all will be before long. Can you bed us down, Bart?"

"If you don't mind spare comfort."

The pauses were longer, but silence was beneficent. Like a solvent, it took away self-consciousness and seemed to give them a chance to be themselves. Need had made a miscellaneous group into a family. The protective disguises they had been wearing were slipping away.

Helen's brittleness had given way to a concern she had not known herself capable of feeling; but then she had never had a small baby to fuss over. Wondering what she had missed, she pushed the thought away and decided to

38

get what pleasure she could out of this one experience.

Vera's lack of interest in life was lessening. She found herself responding to the challenge of ideas. Under the pressure to keep going, to keep up with a trend she had not really liked, she had lost energy and with it all interest. Now something was stirring within her. It was a little like the feeling she had had when she first realized there was life in her womb: a life unplanned, thought unwanted, but a life to be reckoned with.

Val, steeped in cynicism, could not find the way of relinquishment even for a few hours as the others seemed to be finding. He knew he had been well fed, that he was warm, safe from the elements. Perhaps, just perhaps, he told himself, he might begin to see a reason behind the mystery, the mystery that because it baffled him had led to rejection. An inner door had been closed for so long that he had become used to negating anything that tried to open it. Now—and it appeared to be against his will—the door was being pushed open. He might have to reconsider some of his attitudes, but not yet, not yet. Even as he said the words inwardly, the door yielded a little. The bolt was not as strong as he had thought it was.

"Bart, you've given us Amy's philosophy. How about your own?"

"Mine?" Bart looked at Gabe and his tone said clearly, "How could anyone be interested in mine?" He turned to Martin to help him out.

Martin's memory was clear. "Remember the old stone in the graveyard in England? One of our parishioners sent you a picture of it on a postcard."

Bart was puzzled, then a smile broke over his face. "Everybody knows those words."

"I don't," Val said.

Bart repeated them slowly: " 'God give me work til my life shall end, and life till my work is done.' "

8:00 P.M.

"Thanks, that should be enough for anyone," Val admitted, surprising himself that for once he felt in some kind of agreement. "The trouble with me is that I've never been able to find my work."

Martin glanced at Val, wondering how hard he had tried.

Gabe, looking at Bart's weathered face and at the hands that still had strength in them, said, "I guess work hasn't hurt you any."

"Might as well like what has to be done if you're the one who's going to do it."

"And so make your life your prayer," Martin added.

"I can remember only one prayer, the one I learned when I was a little boy," Gabe said taking up Martin's remark. Then he repeated the words hesitantly, as if he had not said them for a long time: " 'Now I lay me down to sleep, I pray the Lord my soul to keep, and if I die before I wake, I pray the Lord my soul to take.' "

No one made any comment, so Gabe continued, "Can't say that it's done anything for me except to take away a congenital fear of death."

"That's something."

"If I say it now"—Gabe paused as if the words were inward—"I feel all right about tomorrow."

Martin brought his hands together as a cat will its paws when catching a fly, only for him it was an idea. "You've got something, Gabe, and it's a workable philosophy, but you haven't recognized it as such. Good old Jeremy Taylor said it was an art to die well and that it should be learned by men in health."

Gabe beamed at Martin's compliment. "Thanks, but I'm not sure that I get the connection."

"Simply this: that by eliminating any fear of death while realizing that it will come, you free yourself to live one day at a time."

Silver Lining

Gabe started to reply but was cut short by Helen's observation.

"If I've a rule to live by, it's to live without fear. My father got that through to me when I was a little girl —teaching me to swim, then to dive; teaching me to ride, then to jump. I was often scared, but he'd say to me, 'Do the thing you fear to do and it will be the end of fear.' And so it was." She turned toward Bart. "Don't think I wasn't afraid this evening when I locked the car and started up the road toward your light with my overnight case. Whatever was I getting myself in for! Then I heard my father's voice, as I've heard it countless times across the years, and I knew I had to face up to my fear."

41

"You certainly acted confident when you arrived on my doorstep."

"Oh, I can act."

Gabe said, "I suppose it's the storm outside and the security within, but we're letting each other into our hearts as we'd never do under ordinary conditions."

Val stirred. "If Vera weren't sound asleep and hemming me down, if the weather hadn't locked us in, I'd get up and walk out on you all. Your chatter bores me. I've no feeling for life. I don't care for it any more than it cares for me."

"The 'ifs' of history," Bart murmured. "What would have happened if—if—if—all down the ages, but the fact remains that the 'ifs' didn't happen. The storm has enclosed us all, your wife has fallen asleep—"

"She's not my wife."

"But she is the mother of your child."

"Yes."

Bart looked at Val's face, or as much of it as he could see, hidden as it was by the long hair that fell forward as he leaned toward the stove. It was a fine face, sensitive, intelligent. Once the tumult of youth was left behind, and the gloom of aimlessness, something was bound to assert

8:00 P.M.

itself. And he had Vera. Bart told himself that they must love each other or they wouldn't have stayed together, if not as husband and wife then as man and woman.

Val, aware of an atmosphere new to him even though he was not in sympathy with it, felt moved to share the decision he and Vera had come to earlier that day. "This afternoon, Vera and I made a suicide pact. There just didn't seem any reason for either one of us to go on living. We planned to leave Baby at the first house we passed, then go off into the woods for our rendezvous with death."

Helen gasped. The others listened silently.

"The house down by the road looked empty and we saw the light from this one, so we came up the hill, slipping and sliding and cursing our luck. When we got to the porch, the dog barked. Before we could get Baby out of the carrier to leave her on the porch, knocking first so someone would know she was there, the door opened, and you asked us to come in." Val lifted his head, pushed back his hair and looked at Bart. "And we came, all three of us."

As if exhausted by all he had said, or freed by it, Val eased his thin body down beside Vera's and put one arm under his head and the other around her. Drawing her to him, he closed his eyes and gave the appearance of sleep.

Bart, gazing at them, thought how Amy would have loved them.

For a long time no one said anything. The clock could be heard ticking. The dog snuffled occasionally, wood whispered in the stove, the rocker creaked. Outside, the snow continued to fall.

"It's hardly fair to us, Pastor, to ask you for the philosophers' stone that you roll around in your pocket, but—"

"Why not, Gabe?"

"You'll give us a dose of theology, and some of us aren't ready for that now, or ever."

Silver Lining

"Quite the contrary, my dear fellow. I've been sitting here listening and thinking how much you've been giving me. Everything's grist to my mill, and much of what I've heard tonight will be cropping up in my sermons during the next few months."

"You mean it?"

Martin nodded, a puckish smile forerunner of his words. "Compared with you young people, I'm a rank hedonist. Life has been something that I have found enjoyable, increasingly so. The stone I roll around in a pocket of my mind is to hold fast to the good, and in rejecting the wrong do what I can to right it."

"What about the changes that take place with the years?"

"Change? It's one of life's conditions. Learn to accept it."

"And the end?"

"A door opening."

"It's because you're a religious that you feel that way."

"Perhaps."

Val sighed. He was not asleep. "Oh, my G—." His words went down the scale. Unheard or unheeded, they remained with him.

Martin went on. "There was a time when I didn't know how I got into this world or why, but finding out some things has given meaning to me. Now I feel like a debtor who has received unwarranted riches. The way I live my life is the way I pay my debt."

"I feel just the other way," Gabe said. "Because I'm here, life owes me something."

"Here lies one who had nothing to say to life," Val murmured, "so life said nothing to him."

"But you did say something to life," Helen spoke up sharply. "You have a child."

"Not intentionally."

8:00 P.M.

"Whether you wanted her or not is no matter now. You set in motion the means of her arriving here."

"God help her," Val groaned and put his arm over his face, retreating again into his semblance of sleep.

"He will," Martin said.

Almost as if on cue, Baby let out a long wail, a diminuendo of misery. Jock stood up slowly, unsteadily, then dropped his head to lap the small face that was screwing itself up for another release of sound.

Vera said sleepily, "She's wet."

Helen, rather liking her role of surrogate mother, trotted across the room. "I'll take care of her." Soon she had picked up the baby. Resting the red head against her shoulder, she patted the little damp behind and went into the bedroom. "I'll have to use another one of your towels, Bart," she called back.

"Help yourself."

Jock looked around as he came out of his oblivion. Finding a focus for his eyes on the only one he knew, he padded across the room to stand beside Bart. Resting his long nose on Bart's knee, he gazed up at him. Bart knew the suppliant look.

"He wants his supper." Getting up, Bart went to the pantry followed by the dog; both of them moved slowly, stiff from the long time they had been still.

Martin followed Helen into the bedroom, not because he felt competent to help her, but because he could not resist a baby or any small thing: the helplessness and the potential.

Gabe strolled to the door. Opening it, he went out to stand on the porch. Enjoying the ranging conversation at first, he had begun to weary of it as it seemed to be getting nowhere. In spite of bodily comfort and friendly people, he felt restlessness coming over him. Then he saw what he had not noticed when he arrived—the tools hanging from

the wall of the house and the snowshoes. It was like the old
man to be prepared, Gabe thought. He looked at the snow
and tried to estimate its depth. Ten inches, or twelve,
perhaps, but it had stopped, or nearly so, and it would
settle some. When daylight came, he and Val would take
turns with the shovel and clear a track down to the road.
But why wait for Val? There was nothing to stop him from
opening his own path and getting down to the road before
anyone was awake.

He turned his attention back to the snowshoes. They
had seen wear, but unfamiliar as they were to him, they
looked in traveling condition; even the harnesses had
been kept oiled and were supple. Gabe ran his hands over
and around them. Not now, but early in the morning after
the first plows had cleared the state road and while the
others were still dozing, he would take the snowshoes and
get down to his motorbike. Once free of snow, he would
push it the two miles to Hemphill, get the tire fixed, and be
on his way. Relieved at this prospect, he felt able to return
to the warm room and engage in more talk. Or he might
find a book to read. Anything that would keep him from
thinking. It was thinking that made him impatient. The
hurry that had been driving him for days had released its
hold only momentarily. He hoped he could get through the
rest of the night without its pressure. When morning came
he would be off and away, doing something, going somewhere, putting distance between him and the guilt that
hounded him.

Val and Vera were the only persons in the room when
Gabe returned, and they were involved in a low-voiced
conversation that ruled out any interruption. Gabe tiptoed
over to the bookshelf. A roaming glance at the books made
him feel that he could easily spend what was left of the
night with one or another of them. Some had Bart's name
in them, some Amy's, some both names. Many had pas-

8:00 P.M.

sages underlined and marginal notations. Gabe put six on the floor and sat down beside them, ready for a dialogue, not only with the writers of the books, but also with the two who had read and responded to them.

"I'd feel better, Val, if you asked him to do it."

"I don't get you, Vera. You've never had any use for anything religious, and now, just because there's a pastor around, you want Baby to be christened."

"He might say baptized."

"Oh, well, whatever. It's the same thing."

"It's not just because there's a pastor around, it's because—" She stopped.

He stared at her.

"It's because a name will somehow link her to life, her life."

"This afternoon, when we were making our plans, you didn't have much use for life."

"I'm seeing things differently now. Don't ask me to explain, Val, but something about the storm outside and the peace within and those two old men have given me a new feeling. It's as if life were precious, could be, anyway. If we can't find it for ourselves, perhaps our child will."

"And you think a name will give her a chance?"

Vera nodded. "It will mean we cared."

"Have you thought of one?"

"Zoe."

"Zoe! That's an odd name."

"For her it's right. Life. Please, Val, let's ask Pastor Martin as soon as he comes back."

"There's no hurry. We'll be here until morning."

She threw her arms around him and let her lips melt onto his. He shifted his position so his arms could encircle her. Their pressure tightened, but she wanted it to be even tighter. Once before there had been such a moment; as if they had stepped outside their own selves and become subservient to a force that was using them for an end beyond their knowing.

"Oh my, I'm so happy," Vera whisper-sobbed against him.

"So am I." Val found her lips again.

Bart, returning from the pantry, saw them and enjoyed the sight. They were in no danger of seeing him, and the only other occupant of the room was lost in a book. Bart smiled. Amy would have said that everything was all right between them. He began to move quietly around the room, doing the small chores the hour demanded.

He added another chunk of wood to the stove, added more oil to the lamp. He went back to the pantry for the bottle of milk and a piece of buttered bread so there might be something for the baby. He placed more apples and some pears in a bowl. Opening a chest that stood against the far wall, he brought out a collection of blankets and an assortment of pillows, enough for those who would sleep rolled up on the floor. From the cupboard he took out the glasses and set them on the table near the lamp in case anyone was thirsty. Last, he went to the porch for the jug of spring water that had been cooling there.

The night air was refreshing, and Bart let if flow into the room. As his eyes gradually became accustomed to the darkness, he saw that the snow had stopped. There were no stars to be seen, but he did not doubt that they would appear. The wind had shifted; it was coming in from the north now, the clearing quarter. Feeling it lightly, ever so lightly, he welcomed it. The storm that had been fast moving would pass over as rapidly as it had come. As the wind picked up it would free the oak of some of the weight of snow resting on it. Standing with his back to the room and his eyes peering into the darkness, Bart heard the clock and waited, counting the twelve strokes as they invaded the silence.

8:00 P.M.

MIDNIGHT

IT WAS as if the clock had called them all together. When Bart moved back into the room with the jug of water, he saw Helen in the rocker by the stove. She was bouncing Baby on her knee, and the child's delight sounded like a continuation of the clock's cheerful chiming. Martin was beside her. Gabe was standing nearby, his fingers marking a place in a book as if waiting to read aloud from it. Val and Vera had resumed their back-to-back position. Her hand rested in his, and she was smiling.

Jock was the last to return to the room. It had taken him longer than usual to finish his meal; Bart had given him more than usual, and Jock was a good finisher. After he had run his tongue around and over the dish, he would sniff at the floor in the hope that a crumb might have escaped him and could be located; the final gesture was that of licking his chops. He was doing this as he came from the pantry, but once across the threshold he stopped abruptly. His tail rose like a plume, his ears cocked. A low rumbling came from his throat.

48

It was the sound that drew attention to him. To those unfamiliar with the ways of dogs it seemed threatening.

"What's the matter with your dog, Bart?"

"That's the way he acts when he wants to alert me."

"There couldn't possibly be anyone at the door," Gabe said, "the snow's too deep."

"I don't want anybody else, do you, Val?" Vera looked over her shoulder. "We're just getting to know each other."

"It's the wind, Jock, coming down the mountain," Bart explained; then he told the others about the night—the deep snow but the fact that it had stopped, the cloud covering that was already tearing apart so that stars would soon be appearing, and the shift of wind that was the promise for the morning. Bart made a clicking sound, and Jock came toward him, stepping nimbly around the group by the stove, almost leaping the last space to reach the outstretched hand and start licking it.

"Good fellow." Bart rubbed Jock's head and fondled his ears. They understood each other no matter what anyone else might think or say.

"Bart, we're got a favor to ask of you and Pastor Martin," Vera began.

"Yes?"

Val continued, "We'd like to have our daughter baptized tonight, and we'd like you to stand up as her godfather. Helen, will you be her godmother?"

Bart nodded slowly. Helen accepted with a flurry of pleasure. Martin smiled. "If you have a name, I'll be glad to see it become hers in the traditional way."

Preliminaries were soon attended to. Helen had insisted on brushing the baby's hair and tidying her up before she placed her in Vera's arms; then they all grouped around the table, the lamplight on their faces.

Gabe's eyes were on the jug. "Water," he said, to no one

Midnight

in particular, "not chlorinated, not fluoridated, just pure water."

"She's a rosebud if there ever was one," Martin said and touched the baby's cheeks, then bent down to kiss her.

Drowsy but aware that something had made her the center of attention, the child smiled blissfully, then closed her eyes. The fingers that had been curled tightly into her palms relaxed; the hands opened, revealing lines of life. Vera touched her lips to the child's, and Val did the same. They looked at each other. It was a proud moment. The defeat and despair that had companioned them for so long had gone. Each knew that the reprieve might be short, but while it lasted they sensed a second chance: if not for them, then for their daughter.

"Can you get on without a book, Martin?" Bart asked.

"My dear man, don't think I need a book for something I've already done a thousand times. I'll ask you and Helen to repeat some words after me, then I'll avail myself of this spring water. Pour some into a bowl, if you please, so it will be warm from the heat of the room and won't be the shock that water sometimes is." He looked at the parents. "I do need a name."

"Zoe," Vera said promptly.

"Zoe," Val repeated.

"Zoe!" Gabe exclaimed. "That's Greek for *life*."

"Couldn't think of anything better," Val said, "since that's what we gave her."

"And now we're giving her to life," Vera added, holding the baby more closely as she spoke.

Martin began the ritual, then turning to Helen told her the words to be repeated. She said them carefully, with a solemnity she felt to be their due.

Martin turned to Bart, whose repetition of the words was anything but solemn.

Silver Lining

"I baptize thee, Zoe, in the name of the Father and all that is good in his creation of which you are a part."

Water sprinkled on the red hair and falling over the flushed cheeks surprised Zoe. Eyelids trembled, lashes lifted. She smiled first at her mother; then the smile embraced them all. One after another smiled back at Zoe, then at each other. Gabe reached out to touch her as if to assure himself that she was real.

"She's sleepy," Vera said.

Bart gestured to the blankets he had collected. Val took one and made a nest of it in a corner of the room. Vera went to the packframe leaning near the door where it had been placed and took from it a small sleeping bag. Shaking it out, she made sure that it was dry, then zipped Zoe into it and placed her in the nest Val had prepared. Almost immediately, Jock drew up. Nosing Zoe in her blanket, he stretched himself out beside her, making a warm wall of protection.

"She'll probably sleep through the night," Vera said as she and Val joined the others still standing around the table. Bart, filling the glasses, offered the first one to Vera. "At this moment, my dear," he said, facing her, "the evening belongs to you and Val. Won't you be the ones to give the toast to which we all may drink?"

Vera held her glass and looked into it as if the words were there and would rise of their own volition into utterance. She turned to Val. He held his glass toward the lamp, then in a courtly gesture made a bow with it to each one. To Vera, standing beside him, he touched his glass against hers.

"The conventional thing might be to drink to a long life and a merry one for the small Zoe who has now retreated into sleep," Val said, "but I think her mother and I would like to feel that she will find meaning in life, however long

51

Midnight

or short hers may be. So—" he lifted his glass high—"to a meaningful life!" He put the glass to his lips, and the others followed his lead and drank from theirs.

"To a meaningful life!" Each one repeated the toast.

Bart took the empty jug and the glasses to the pantry and was followed by Martin.

Helen and Vera sat down in two of the chairs near the stove and were soon caught up in easy conversation. Val strolled over to the bookshelf to see if there was anything that might appeal to him. Gabe started pacing up and down the room. He went to the door, thinking of the snowshoes while knowing that it was no use trying to get away until morning. He went back to the pantry where Bart and Martin were talking together.

"How long till morning, Bart? Till light, I mean."

"Six or seven hours, maybe less, depending a little on the wind."

"How long till the road will be open?"

"Hard to say. That depends on many things. Could be several hours."

Gabe stared. Annoyed by Bart's calm words and Martin's bland expression, he spoke sharply, "I want to get out."

Bart moved his head in the direction of the bedroom.

"No, no, not that. I want to get going. I want to do something."

"There's a shovel on the porch."

Gabe left the two and went quickly to find his coat and helmet.

Val, without looking up from the book he was reading, said, "Cool it, Gabe. We can't do anything now. Wait until daylight. We'll all pitch in and get a path dug out, unless help gets up to us first, which it well may."

"Maybe there won't be any morning."

"So what?"

Gabe whistled between his teeth. "That's all you care."
He put his hand on the door and opened it, but after a
glance at the whiteness of the outer world he drew back.

"Change your mind?"

Gabe threw himself down on the floor beside Val. "I
can't stand doing nothing." His voice rose, not in petu-
lance but in anger.

"We're better off than we'd be in a snowbank," Helen
reminded him, shuddering at the thought of what her own
situation would be now had she holed herself up in her
car.

"I want to get out—to get going!" Gabe's words were a
crescendo that ended in a sob of frustration.

"Please," Vera said, her voice subdued, "don't wake
Zoe or we'll not have any quiet."

"We're trapped," Gabe cried, "like animals."

"Just because you feel that way, don't put it on all of us.
Vera and I haven't had it so comfortable in a long time."

Martin and Bart came from the pantry. Martin went to
Gabe and stood looking down at him. "Maybe we're all
feeling the same way, Gabe," he said quietly, "closed in,
kept from our usual procedures, but there isn't anything
any one of us can do until morning."

"We may all be dead by then."

"What if we are?"

The tone of Martin's voice shocked Gabe as if cold water
had been thrown on him. He stared up at the pastor and
demanded, "Don't you care?"

"Of course I care, but there are other things I care about
more. One of them is peace of mind and another is consid-
eration. Come along." He bent down and slipped his arm
under Gabe's, helping him stand up. "Let's go into the
other room where we can talk together."

Gabe had no intention of going with him. Irritated by
the apparent unconcern of the older people and infuriated

at the way his contemporaries had fallen into complacence, he shook himself free of the pastor's hold.

Martin knew what a man in panic could do. He did not like to think of what might happen to them all in the close confinement of Bart's house if Gabe lost his self-control. He reached for Gabe's hand and grasped it. "Come along, Gabriel, you and I have many things to talk about, and time is short. Let's not waste any more of it."

Gabe, startled by the use of his full name in such a decisive tone and compelled by the firm hold Martin had on his hand, went with him into the bedroom.

Martin pushed the door to behind them. For a time the room, as far as he was concerned, would have the sanctity of his study. A man didn't act as Gabe had just been acting unless he had something pressing on his mind, and Martin wanted to make it possible for Gabe to loosen up and let go whatever it was that troubled him. A candle on the dresser gave light to the room. Martin, familiar with candles, guessed that it had about an hour's burning; not enough to last until morning, but there was undoubtedly another candle to take its place.

He put pressure on Gabe's arm so he would sit on the bed. Martin sat in a small straight chair near the window. The room was cold, but it was bracing after the warmth of the living room. He looked at the window. Upon the glass frost had made a delicate, intricate design. He told himself that he might have been in a church whose rose window was not multicolored but diamondlike in its tracery.

"Now," he said, folding his hands comfortably across his ample middle, "I've a chance to go back and try to recall where it is we've met, for your face is surely familiar to me."

Gabe made no reply. It gave him a measure of self-confidence to keep the old man guessing. They had never met, but if the cat-and-mouse game they were playing

Silver Lining

offered the pastor some amusement, Gabe could afford him the time. There was nothing else to do.

"Guess on," Gabe said, knowing he could demolish any guess, knowing he had never seen Martin Amblin before and willing to trust his memory and eyesight rather than the older man's.

Their talk was casual. All Martin wanted to do was put Gabe at ease. Long experience had taught him that once rapport was established something might be said that would open the way for deeper talk. So they spoke about books and studies. Martin recalled his years as a seminarian, realizing that what had happened to him forty years ago would sound like the dark ages to a young man who couldn't be more than twenty-two.

"And you never doubted that you were on the right track, doing the right thing, making yourself the servant of a God who doesn't exist except in people's minds?"

"Can you think of a better place to exist than in the mind?"

Gabe shrugged off the question and returned to his own first question: "You never doubted?"

"Of course I doubted—all the time—and I wouldn't be here today as I am if I hadn't. Doubt is one of the healthiest of states for a young mind, or for any mind."

"I don't get you."

"It means you won't settle for a semblance of truth. You compel yourself to go on toward the whole. And it wasn't any theologian's view or any treatise that helped me through my doubts. It was my own hard thinking that convinced me that I would make my confrontation with God or none would be made."

"God!" Gabe exclaimed with an edge of annoyance, "let's leave Him out of this."

"Can't, my dear fellow, and have anything left, for God is life."

Midnight

"Not a man in the sky?" Gabe's expression was that of a little boy teasing a slow-witted adult.

It pleased Martin as an indication that the moment of madness had been relieved.

"You surprise me, Gabriel. Anthropomorphism went out of style a long time ago. When I use the word you query, I mean the immense Being in whom we live and move and are."

Gabe's head lifted abruptly. "Who said that?"

"Many people have in different ways, down the ages. I'm saying it now."

It was the lift of the head that did it, the angle of light on the face that established recognition. Martin knew now where he had seen that face. It was unmistakable—the high cheekbones, the slightly teasing smile, the hair curling back from the brow like that of an ancient Greek.

"I'm not sure that I like your calling me Gabriel."

"Sorry, but I probably shall continue. It's a noble name, and a man should use his name.

"Glad you said use and not live up to."

"There may not be an appreciable difference."

Gabe tossed off the observation and talked on. As he did, he became more like the jaunty individual who had arrived at Bart's door a few hours earlier than the man obsessed with a need to get away and get going. Martin waited for his moment, not wanting to do anything precipitate that would disturb their newfound relationship. Gabe's words were a diatribe against one of his college courses when Martin suddenly interrupted him.

"I know where I've seen you—in the post office!"

Gabe laughed at the absurdity. "Couldn't possibly. I don't live in these parts, and you told me you hadn't left this valley for years."

Unperturbed, Martin leaned back in his chair and smiled. "That's where it was, only you didn't see me."

Gabe's expression was still mocking. His lips parted as if to speak again in denial; then his lips froze and he stared at Martin.

The pastor knew Gabe could lie; he was capable of it. He knew he could leave the room in a huff, go out the front door and plunge into the snow; or he could stay where he was and face a fact.

The pause lengthened. Gabe's lips closed, and he dropped his gaze. If it went anywhere it was to the floor. When he finally spoke he did not look up.

"You mean—the picture?"

"Yes, and it's a very good one, but your hair was dark as I recall."

Gabe nodded. "You read what it said?"

"Yes, I always read those notices. They give me people to pray for at night when I can't sleep."

"Then you've prayed for me?"

"Indeed I have."

"In spite of what I did—what I'm wanted for?"

"Yes, dear boy, but that's not important now. What's done is done. I prayed that you would find yourself while there was still time."

"Time?"

"Yes, or life. The words in this case are somewhat simi-lar." Martin spoke slowly, gently, as if to a small child whose attention he had at last gained and did not want to lose. It was a portion of his own philosophy that he gave to Gabe. "Life well lived, and that *well* includes repentance and restitution, makes one ready for death: ready to accept it as the next logical step."

Gabe shot a swift glance at him. "Then you think we're not going to come out of this night alive, and you want to make me ready to—"

Martin moved his hand lightly as if to wave away what had been misinterpreted. "Our lives are no more precari-

Midnight

ous on one day than another, Gabriel. To be ready for whatever happens: this is the challenge and the test. To be ready and yet to be surprised."

There was a pause, far longer than any of the other pauses between them, but Martin had a feeling that they had not come to the end of all there was to say.

"I've been running away," Gabe began, "ever since I did it, trying to put distance between me and the law, trying to blot out the memory."

"It's not the law you're running from, Gabriel, but your conscience, and it will be with you all your life. Face up, pay the price whatever it may be, and you're a free man."

"I may have a jail sentence."

"Even so. In yourself you'll be free."

Gabe's eyes met Martin's and his gaze held steady. "I've wanted to get away, but now—" he looked dazed, unbelieving"—but now I'm beginning to want to go back."

"You can be the first one to use the snow shovel when morning comes."

"Once I get *Bucephalus* fixed I'll head back to California and give myself up."

"You won't have to go that far; every post office has your picture. You can turn yourself in at Hemphill." Martin stood beside Gabe, sitting on the edge of the bed, and placed his hands on Gabe's curly hair. "Live worthy of the name you were given, Gabriel."

Gabe shook his head with a swift violent motion, and Martin's hands fell away. Suddenly a fierce desire raged in him to be rid of everything—the room, the people, the talk. He wanted to leave it all behind him, go through the door, plunge into the snow, and even without *Bucephalus* dare the world again. He was young, he was strong, he had proved himself clever enough to evade the law. He could still do so. His breath came in quick short gasps. He felt as if he were drowning, fighting for air. And he knew he was drowning in a fact he could not escape, would never be able to escape as long as he lived. Anguished, he put his head in his hands, rocking it back and forth.

"Oh, G—," he groaned.

Martin said nothing.

"Can you—" Gabe muttered through the hands that covered his face "—can you give me some kind of assurance that I'll be able to live with myself again? Ever?"

Martin took Gabe's hands away from his face and held them firmly in his own hands. It was a long moment. Finally Gabe raised his eyes and looked at Martin. When he spoke he answered his own question. "It's up to me, isn't it?"

Martin nodded slowly, and only then did he let go the hold he had on Gabe's hands.

Gabe sighed. A thin smile made his lips quiver. "You know something? I wouldn't be surprised if there were a God."

"Surprised? Not by the fact but by the ways of the working."

Gabe stood up. "This room is cold. Don't you want to join the others by the stove?"

"Yes, soon. I'm just going to sit here for a while. I rather fancy what the light from the candle is doing to that frost tracery on the window glass."

In the arch manner that came easily to him, Gabe said, "I bet you're going to pray." But the teasing tone was pleasant, that of the little boy who had yielded a point but couldn't resist a last word.

"And you pray, too, Gabriel, the prayer you learned long ago and that has stood by you."

"Thanks, Pastor Martin."

Midnight

Gabe left the room, and Martin returned to the chair by the window. Inwardly he said, as he did often, "Don't thank me, thank God."

Martin looked at the window, there was no looking through it. Ferns that never grew, fountains that never flowed were etched on the glass. Warm air meeting cold air had resulted in beauty. Wonder and worship were familiars to him, and he felt both as he observed what the movement of air had done. Then he told himself that the air could not have created such beauty had there not been something to work on: the pane of glass. Would anything have happened had there not been a meeting of opposites?

His meditation was interrupted by Val's voice at the door. "Mind if I join you?"

Martin smiled a welcome and gestured to the bed to sit on.

"That room is hot and the talk's hot, too. Bart and Helen are on the political situation, and to my amazement Vera is right in there with them. I never thought she cared what went on in the world."

Martin had no rejoinder so he kept silent.

"What's ahead for us, Pastor?"

"I thought that was the kind of speculative discussion that drove you from the tropics to this arctic chamber."

Val gave the door a kick with his foot. It closed with a soft sucking sound as if it had opened and closed so often that it had learned to perform its office agreeably. "No, not the big world outside, the little one here where we are for this one night."

Martin gave a lift to his shoulders as if to imply that Val's guess was as good as his.

Val acted like a man who had suddenly come awake to a situation through which he had long been drowsing. "Are we going to get out of this all right?"

Silver Lining

Again the shoulders hunched; again the smile crept over Martin's face. "That's a question we can ask ourselves any day on waking: "What of tonight? Only in the case of all of us here we say: "What of the morning?"

Val sighed as if he thought he might never get an answer to his question. He glanced around the room. It was small and square with no more in it than a bedroom required. Near the one window the only chair was occupied. On the dresser, catching light from the candle, was a photograph of an older woman. Near the bed was a shelf with a few books on it. "I want to know," Val said.

"You're not the only one, but why, Val?"

"Because I've discovered that I want to live. I think it's the first time in years that I've felt this way. I—I can't understand what's happened to me."

Martin wished he could look into Val's eyes, but his head was down and the long hair had fallen forward, obscuring his face; he wished he had been near enough to touch the hands that were moving nervously. He would have liked to hold them still. "Whatever happens, Val, you'll live."

"How can you be so sure?"

"Because life is a process that commenced a long time ago, for all of us, and we can't stop it. It will continue."

"That isn't what I mean."

"Granted, but it's something everyone has to face sooner or later."

"It's easy for you because you're—because you've lived longer than most of us here."

"You're not quite right, Val. I think Bart has the advantage there. But, no matter, it isn't years that count."

Val drew in his breath quickly. "I'd never call getting old an advantage."

"No, of course you wouldn't."

Midnight

Val shook his head. He looked at his hands; he looked around the room again; then he brought his gaze back to the man by the window.

"Life is constant discovery," Martin went on, "and all of it is gradual. You'll find, Val, when you get up to 'getting old,' that there are distinct advantages."

"Like what?"

"Things hurt less. You develop a kind of immunity. If you've lived reasonably well, you can be more than reasonably healthy."

"But think of all you can't do! You can't see without glasses, often can't hear without a hearing aid."

"Oh, you are so right! But is what one hears with the ear, sees with the eye all there is to hear and see? There's an inner ear, an inner eye, and each has a way of intensifying with time."

"What about stiffening joints and hearts that can't take strain?"

"There's no denying them, but what takes place, Val, is that one comes into a new rhythm. Mind you, it's been happening gradually, so one goes along with it."

"Don't you resent it?"

"If you do, you get into trouble. Accept it as part of the process—dawn to dusk, spring to winter. In each phase there's something new. I find myself looking ahead with more excitement than I had when I was your age."

"Ahead!" Val's tone was sarcastic. "What's ahead but the obliteration of death?"

"That's what you think."

"Some people take so long to die."

"And there are many for whom we wish death would never come," the pastor rejoined.

Again Val sighed. "I'm getting along about as well with you as when I argue with Vera."

"And that means?"

Silver Lining

"I'm always the one without the answers." Val put his hands up to his long hair and pushed it back behind his ears.

"Pleased to meet you," Martin said, smiling.

"What's that mean?"

Martin chuckled. "Just that now we're face to face. I find it a little difficult to talk with a person whose countenance is curtained from me."

Then Val laughed. "I'll cut it off in the morning. That will please Vera. She says it gets in her way."

"Val," Martin said, leaning toward him, "nobody has the answers. All that any of us can do is keep discovery alive. And be expectant."

"That's my trouble. I'm lazy. I'd rather sit down and bemoan my lot—the lot of my generation—than stand up and do anything about it."

"We can't stay sitting down, Val, we have to keep going."

There was a pause, then Val spoke slowly. "I'm getting the idea. I'm even beginning to want in when for so long I've wanted out."

"Because of Zoe."

"Not entirely."

Again there was a pause, so long this time that it might have seemed a point had been reached where words were no longer needed.

"We're thinking of going to see Vera's folks. They have a farm in Kansas. I might even find work there. I've a feeling for the land. We both have."

Martin smiled. Then they had been making plans when they were whispering together, lying on their backs by the stove. "Give time a chance, Val."

"That's what we want to do."

"Remember what Bart said about the pears?"

"You mean the ripening?"

Midnight

"Yes. As different in its way for each one of us as it is for the fruits of the earth. The pear falls, the apple is picked, the grapes are harvested, each when it is ready; and it is time that has made them so, time working with sun and rain and thrusts of wind. For us it is much the same, living through the good times and the hard, responding to challenges. Readying. Ripening."

Val looked thoughtful. "Maybe it doesn't matter so much where we are or what we're doing so long as that ripening goes on."

"Maybe it doesn't matter."

During the silence that followed, Val got up and left the room.

The door remained open unless intentionally shut, and the warmth that streamed in was welcome to the man sitting by the window. He could hear the talk: Gabe was holding forth, Vera was questioning, Helen exclaiming. Bart's succinct comments were like periods, and after them the conversation moved into new areas. Val's voice was not heard. He's listening, Martin thought, catching up with them. Martin turned his gaze back to the tracery on the glass. That it could be, and be so utterly beautiful, was a mystery. He did not want it explained to him. A meditative moment was in itself a mystery.

"Prefer your own company?"

Roused from reverie, Martin saw Helen standing in the doorway. "Never, if it's you I can share time with." He stood. "But it's rather cold in this room."

Helen settled herself on the bed and tucked a blanket around her. "You're a charmer, Pastor Martin. Ever since I met you I've been thinking how fortunate the ministry is to have someone like you."

"And me to have the ministry."

Helen pointed to the picture on the dresser. "Tell me about her."

Silver Lining

"Amy?"

"Yes. What was she like?"

"She reminded me of a tree. No matter how the years added up or what they held, she remained true to her essential nature."

Martin's thoughts went back over the years he had known the Wilmers, come to their home, been made to feel a part of their lives. "She was a woman of great dignity, but plain; of much wisdom, but a native wisdom; if you know what I mean."

"I think I do."

"They were made for each other. Their minds met, their hearts matched, and both deepened with the years."

"Did she look like her picture when she died?"

Martin turned his gaze back to the picture. "Yes, Amy didn't change much. She only became more so; again, if you know what I mean."

"I'm not sure."

"She lived in the spirit."

"That's a cryptic description."

Martin seemed surprised. "It's very simple, as everything was about Amy. What she did mattered little; the spirit in which she did it mattered a great deal."

"I should think he would be lost without her, living here alone, with just his dog for company."

Martin studied the face that was at one moment looking at him and at another moment at the photograph on the dresser. "He lives for the time when he'll catch up with her."

Helen was silent, then said impulsively, "You know about me and Dexter?"

"That you were not happy."

"If I had it to do all over again, I—" Helen stopped short.

"The 'ifs' of history! Don't fash yourself now, my dear. It does no good to look back."

Midnight

"But I can't look ahead. There's so little time."

Martin's eyebrows lifted in questioning.

"Ever notice the way it keeps shortening on us? There are not nearly so many minutes in the hour, or hours in the day, as there used to be. I'll probably wake up some morning and find there isn't any time at all."

"And perhaps that's as it should be."

Helen's mood changed. The banter was gone and her tone became serious. "Are we in any danger tonight, cooped up in this small house with all that snow outside?"

"Ask me that in the morning."

"If we are, it won't really matter to me. It will just mean that the end will come for me a little sooner than"—she held her breath a moment—"than expected, and without the pain." She told him what she had been told at the clinic that afternoon. "They gave me six months."

He listened, then moved his chair closer to the bed and took her hands in his. "I knew," he said.

"How did you know?"

"I saw it in your eyes."

She looked away, as if fearful of what else he might see in her eyes. "Good or not so good as it may have been, is one ever ready to let life go?"

"Some people are. Bart is. He's so sure of what's ahead, who's ahead."

"Shall I tell you a secret?" Her gaze came back to meet his.

"I'm very good at keeping them."

"If it should be my last night, it's the happiest I've had in a long time—such an unusual collection of people, such fascinating talk, and that baby!"

"You have a trip planned?" he reminded her.

"Yes, Fiji. The tour starts at LA two weeks from now. I don't know what I'll do with myself between now and then. There's something I ought to do, but I don't know that I can get myself to do it." She looked at him hard; having shared one secret, she decided to share another and launched into a story about Dexter's sister in a nursing home in Denver. Helen had avoided her for years, even though they had once been good friends. Aware of her disapproval at the way the marriage had broken up, Helen had felt unwilling to face her. "I should see her before it's too late, but—" Her voice trailed off into silence.

"Colorado," Martin murmured almost to himself. "Would you be going through Kansas?"

"Every flat and weary mile of it, and they'll be flatter and wearier because I'll be dreading my meeting with Dorothy."

"Like some company?"

She stared at him. "You? Are you going to see someone in Kansas?"

"No, not me."

The clock could be heard chiming.

"Three o'clock!" Helen exclaimed. "I can't believe it. But who—"

"I'll tell you in the morning." He rose and held out his hand as if inviting her to dance a minuet with him. "Shall we join the others?"

Together they went into the next room.

Midnight

3:00 A.M.

W E'VE all but talked the night away," Helen said by way of recognition. "I don't know when I've been up so late."

"You'd think we'd always known each other the way we've been talking."

Gabe agreed with Vera. "It's been a long time since I've been part of a family, two years at least, but I feel tonight as if we were related. How are we going to feel in the morning when we start to dig ourselves out?"

"Why should we feel any different?" Martin asked, then turned to Bart. "How long now to morning?"

"Three hours or so to light, four to sunshine."

"You're sure about the sun?"

"Reasonably so. That sky last evening promised fair weather."

Gabe, who had crossed the room to the door and looked out, had the latest report. "It's blowing."

"We can use some wind, but I'll be glad if it doesn't come on too strong."

"Why, Bart, because of drifting?"

"Yes. When the snow packs, it makes shoveling that much harder."

They began making their sleeping arrangements. Helen was given the bedroom. Val and Vera took their sleeping bags to the corner near the bookshelf. A glance at Zoe assured Vera that she was still nestled in her blanket and in the care of the dog. Bart and Martin took the chairs by the stove and agreed to go on shifts. While one dozed the other would remain awake. Gabe said he didn't think he would sleep.

"Why?"

"Because I want to see the dawn."

"You won't from here," Bart explained. "Equity rises too steep and close. You can see the dawn's reflection on the hills to the west after the sun's been up awhile."

"Get some sleep, Gabriel," Martin said, a warning tone in his voice.

"I'll call you when there's light," Bart promised.

Gabe looked from one to the other uncertainly, then decided to put them both at ease by agreeing to go to sleep. "But you will wake me?"

"With the first light. There's a shovel on the porch so you can start digging us out."

"If that's the case, I'll take a book to bed with me." He made his choice, then took a blanket and spread it on the floor halfway between the stove and the door.

Helen, her hand on the bedroom door, turned back to Martin. "Pastor, may we ask you for a prayer so we'll know that God is with us?"

"Indeed, dear lady, and with pleasure if I may put it the other way around, so we will know that we are ever with God." He closed his eyes, was silent for a moment, then spoke as if to a friend.

"Thank you for the warmth and comfort of this home

3:00 A.M.

that Bart and Amy Wilmer have for so long shared with others. Thank you for bringing us together out of the storm. As we turn to rest that we may be ready for the morrow, may each one of us know that whatever the morrow brings we are in your care."

The first Amen came from Helen; the others followed.

Martin, opening his eyes, looked at them and smiled. "He giveth his beloved sleep."

To at least one member of the group the words had a familiar ring. Some had never heard them before, but each one took them as a hint of blessing through the hours of darkness.

Bart lowered the wick in the lamp, checked the damper in the stove, then sat down in the chair beside Martin. The room was quiet. Soon there was the sound of even breathing that told of at least three sleepers. "It's good to sit down," Bart said, "to relax into the calm of a contemporary."

"You've been pretty much on the go one way or another ever since the first wayfarer turned up at your door."

Bart agreed. "It will be different now for a while. In a few minutes I'll go up to the attic and open one of the windows for some air. The room is almost too warm and close."

"Time enough for that when I doze off, which is going to be soon." Martin sighed contentedly. "Nice, isn't it, to be able to be ourselves, two old friends sitting by a warm stove."

"The only time I ever feel old, Martin, or am aware of my years, is when I try to combat the disillusionment of youth."

As they talked together about the young people, Martin said that he felt the night had become a turning point in their lives. "They're different, Bart, from when they came through your door, driven by the weather. It's as if they'd

found something precious, something worth living toward."

"And Helen?"

"She has as much ahead of her, when morning comes, as
the others have. As you have, Bart."

"Maybe there won't be any morning for me, Martin."

Martin let Bart's words sink and settle into the silence.
He waited, but there were no more. "I'll challenge you, my
friend, on what you've just said. No matter how wishful
we may feel, or even expectant, we cannot say the when. It
is one of life's mysteries."

"I'm ready." Bart's tone implied finality.

"But willing?" Martin's smile was quizzical.

"Same thing, aren't they?"

"No." Martin paused, then went on. "To be ready is the
ideal state prescribed for us at all times; to be willing is to
be acceptant of whatever happens."

Bart shook his head in disagreement. "I feel I've done
just about all I can do."

"Just about." Martin picked up Bart's words and handed
them back to him. "There may be one more thing or a
dozen, Bart, and the decision isn't yours." He wagged his
finger at his friend as he had earlier at Gabe. "Don't be
lured, Bartholomew, and think you can get out so easily.
You might slip into a descent, and when a man does that
he's done for. Life is to live, that's all there is to it, and it's
uphill all the way. Has it ever been otherwise?"

"Is this the way you've been talking to the others who
sought you out when you were in the small room?"

"We exchanged ideas. Perhaps I conveyed some of my
own feelings, and I listened. There's not one of them, even
the one now sleeping in your bed, who isn't seeking something."

"Or Someone."

3:00 A.M.

"Definitely." Martin held his hands out as if holding an invisible substance between them. "When you get a group such as we have been tonight, held between two segments of time—the known past and the unknown future —essentials are all that matter. It's not surprising that they spoke their thoughts readily."

"And eased their minds."

"Yes, in a manner of speaking, yes."

The gaps in their conversation began to lengthen. From time to time, now Bart, now Martin, stole a sideways glance at the other to see if sleep had come, but both were still open-eyed. Martin's head was back against the chair, a half smile curved his lips. Bart leaned forward, elbows on knees, head resting in his hands. He did not trust himself to lean back. Sleep would have come too soon. Martin's words about one more thing or a dozen reminded him that he was still the host, though most of his guests were asleep. One thing he knew he must do was go up to the attic and open a window. The drowsiness overcoming him had more to do with the closeness of the room than with a need for sleep.

He glanced at his friend. If Martin had dozed off, it would have been a good time to go upstairs. Martin's eyes were closed, but his lips were moving as if in prayer. Bart felt relieved. No need to worry that Martin would fall asleep while he was praying. Perhaps, Bart told himself, if I catch forty winks now I'll feel more like going up to the attic. He raised his head, shifted into a comfortable position, and let his head rest against the back of the chair. He wondered if he should say something to Martin about taking a nap, but he was reluctant to interrupt him.

4:OO A.M.

THE WORLD outside the house was quiet under the snow that had fallen. A foot or more had covered the ground; in places where the wind had driven it the depth was greater. It was up to the sills of the windows and had sifted inside through some of the cracks; it was against the door. Small bushes, their shapes completely hidden, looked as if they had been covered by white sheets. Trees bowed under the weight, branches sagged.

Where snow lay, and that was everywhere, there was nothing to mar its surface. The snow imposed silence. Only the merest whisper of sound came from ice-encased boughs when the wind moved down Equity. Following it, puffs of snow shook away from branches and boughs and settled on the white expanse below. The sky was ablaze with stars, winking so that they gave a sense of movement, scintillating as the snow crystals would when the morning sun found them.

Within the house a dim light still gleamed; from the

73

chimney a thin line of smoke rose, losing itself in the night. And over all the sentinel oak brooded, but as a tree it was shapeless. Masked by the snow that had piled up on branches that still bore their summer's weight of leaves, it had become something huge and mysterious: a hovering of white suspended by the strength of the trunk.

5:OO A.M.

THE SILENCE within differed from the silence outside. Wood in the stove had its own way of talking, as did the wick in the lamp and the Swiss clock. The regular breathing of sleeping people was a well-defined sound. All had found a rhythm, but some breathed more heavily than others. There was no doubt about the two men by the stove, heads back and mouths half open. The young man on the floor was lying on his side, head cradled in the curve of an arm. The long-haired couple were locked in their embrace, but the steady heaving of shoulders told of the total takeover of sleep. In the adjoining room, the occupant of the only bed in the house breathed with a quiet regularity.

The dog was awake.

Jock shook himself and yawned, then stood up and surveyed the room. On noiseless pads he commenced his rounds. Pushing his nose down first to the baby in her nest of a blanket, he satisfied himself and moved on to the others. As a young dog herding sheep, he had been accustomed to check his flock actively during the day when they were grazing and silently at night when they had clustered together and were ruminant. When a changing way of life had taken sheep from his charge, he transferred his instincts to human beings.

For years he had two to care for, then just one; but tonight he had a houseful, and he was in his element, especially since there was a small one who needed to be happed. Only one long used to caring for sheep and their lambs knew how that should be done.

Jock went up to his master and pressed his body close to the chair; then he rested his long nose on Bart's knee and looked at the familiar face. His tail wagged expectantly, but as there was no response the movement gradually slowed and Jock went on to the next person. He visited them all in turn but did not linger with any as he had with his master. Then he padded across the room and sniffed at the crack under the door. He pawed gently at it and sniffed again, panting, because the room was warmer than he was used to. For a time, his were the loudest sounds in the room. He went back to the blanket in which Zoe was nestled and poked his nose around in it; then he fastened his teeth into a corner of the blanket and began to drag it across the room toward the door.

So slow, so even, so sure was his tugging that the baby was not disturbed, nor was anyone wakened. Jock pulled the blanket close to the crack under the door, then pushed with his nose until the blanket made a soft wall behind the baby and against which he could lie down. A whimper came from Zoe, and a hand reached out of the sleeping bag as if to find its hold in a new setting. Jock stretched his head toward the hand and licked it until the fingers uncurled and the hand drew itself back.

Jock would have done the same for a lamb missing its mother while he waited for the shepherd to take over.

Silver Lining

6:00 A.M

BART CAME to with a start. It was not the chiming of the little clock, though he was fully aware of it. It was not the gentle but insistent licking of his hand by Jock. It was not the chill creeping in from the edges of the room, since the stove, with no one to tend it, was giving little heat. It was none of these. It was a voice calling his name; a familiar voice yet one that he could not immediately identify. He sat up straight, awake, alert, alive, but stiff from the cramped confines of the chair. He listened, but he did not hear the voice again.

There was a brushing of wind against the window-panes, enough to make them rattle slightly. Bart stood up, then reached quickly for the back of the chair to steady himself. Jock pushed his body weight against his master and whined.

"All right, boy, but give me time." Bart looked around the room and toward the door. Was someone there? Another traveler struggling through the storm? Or men from the highway crew? Was that what he had heard? No, no, the sound had not come from the door. Jock would have barked had someone been there; and if help had come there would have been a hammering on the door and a shouting that would have awakened everyone. Waiting for his head to clear, waiting for some reliability to come to his legs, Bart remained standing by the chair.

He saw the sleepers on the floor; he saw his friend of many years with whom he had sat out the night. Martin's head had now fallen forward, chin to chest; his hands were loosely folded in his lap. Seeing the sleeping people reminded Bart of something he had told himself he must do for them, but what was it? That's the trouble, he chided himself, unless I make a note I just don't remember. He put his hands to his head to steady it, to think.

Slowly a thought struggled through the fog in his mind. Air. That was what they all needed; that was what he had intended to give them. As his mind cleared, recollection came swiftly. He was going up to the attic to open the window under the eaves. Protected by the overhang of the roof, that was one window that would not be blocked by snow. Once he got it open, cold air would flow down and into the room to refresh the sleeping people.

Then he knew whose voice he had heard: it was Amy's, calling him to one last duty, calling him to her.

Bart lifted his head, straightened his shoulders, clenched and unclenched his hands. As he did so, something like the vitality of youth flowed into him, and the crippling years fell away. He patted Jock's head. "I'm all right, old fellow. You take care of them now."

Their eyes met and held: for them both, time dissolved and love remained.

Jock turned and went back to the blanket near the door. Nosing the child, then giving her cheek a gentle lick with his warm tongue, he settled down beside her.

Silver Lining

Bart went through the pantry to the woodshed. The ladder was there that was used to go up to the attic. "I'm coming, Amy," he called.

It would be cold in the attic, and the window used so infrequently might not open easily. He took his heavy parka from the peg on which it hung, put it on and zipped it, then drew the hood over his head. His mittens were in a pocket, but before pulling them on he went back to the pantry for some of the bread that had been saved for breakfast. He put two slices in his pocket. There might be a bevy of birds sheltering from the storm under the eaves, and they would be hungry. Then he returned to the woodshed.

Placing his hands on both sides of the ladder and grasping it firmly, he put his foot on the first rung, then the next foot and the next rung: another and another until he was standing on the fifth rung and could reach with the flat of a mittened hand to push the hatch up and aside. Cold air streamed over and past him like water. He braced himself against the force of it, pausing long enough to breathe deeply and feel its tonic. He clambered up the remaining rungs and heaved himself through the opening into the attic. He remained on his knees; there was no standing tall in the small space, and he crawled across the boards to the window under the eaves.

The glass was not frosted, and Bart told himself that when he got close to the window he would be able to see stars winking at him, even though the sky was beginning to pale. A reach of sky, framed by the arms of the oak, had always been that window's special province. Near it now, he held his breath so it would not steam the glass. Peering out, he looked for stars. Then he saw why none were visible.

The oak's massive limbs, under their weight of snow, had bowed almost to the roof of the house. In awe, and

6:00 A.M.

then in anguish, Bart saw the situation for what it was and what it might be. If the limbs could hold until the wind did its work, snow would slide off them; when the sun came over Equity it would soon melt the ice that had formed on the foliage. If the limbs, especially the one poised almost within reach, could not hold, the house would be in danger. Bart opened the window and prayed for morning.

Listening again for the call that had wakened him, Bart heard something for which he was not listening, something that came from the tree at the place where the limbs canopied. It was a churning, tearing sound, a sound of protest, as if branches were saying they could no longer stand the strain and the trunk was saying it would not let them go.

In a space of time that might have been a second or might have been far longer, Bart, hearing and seeing, knew what he could do. Climbing out of the window, he took his stance on the ledge, glad that it was wide enough, glad that the distance up the roof beam was sufficient for him to stand upright, then he spread-eagled himself against the house. Memory hurtled back to the time when the house was being built and the carpenter working with him had wanted the attic window to be small, but Bart had been firm, saying that a window should always be big enough for a man to get through it.

"Bart, do you need any help?" It was Martin calling.

Wakened by the cold rush of air, he had gone to the shed and realized where Bart was. Standing at the foot of the ladder, he shouted Bart's name, but his voice did not reach the man on the ledge.

Bart stood and waited as the limbs tore at the heart of the tree and the sound of struggle increased. At a time of stress, he told himself, even an ordinary man could be a Samson. Now there was light enough to see the sagging of the limb nearest him. He reached out to catch hold of it.

Silver Lining

His weight on it might be enough to deflect its fall away from the house.

"Amy!" he cried aloud, then flung himself toward the tree. Grasping the limb, he swayed with it, kicking the air as a swimmer caught in a strong current would kick to free himself.

Slowly, as if it had the fullness of time for its final act, the tree started to fall.

The limb to which Bart was clinging veered away from the house, and he was tossed from it into the snow as lightly as a spent leaf. The tearing sound gained in volume and ended in a thud. The house shook with the impact made on the ground. Bricks, toppling from the chimney, had a staccato sound as they tore through the roof and rattled down the opening in the attic floor. Branches clattered as they caught against each other and icebound foliage was shattered; then there was quiet as intense as the collision of sounds: quiet that rested like a covering on the white world as light began to flow over it. Even the predawn wind had blown itself out and the air was still.

The sun, coming over the summit of Equity, brought brilliance to shrouded trees and trackless surfaces and the gaping wound in the oak's trunk. In time sap would gush up and into the wound, but it would not be sap to nurture life. The oak that had weathered two centuries said *Finis* to the morning.

Bart, lying in the snow where the limb in its fall had thrown him, drew his arms in close to his body and tried to move his legs. Sensation began to return and with it consciousness. Shivering uncontrollably, he felt warm and wondered how this could be. Slowly untangling the skein of his thoughts, while his face was pressed against the snow and he lacked the strength to raise his head, he took himself back over what could have happened to put him where he was. Then, like light streaming into darkness of

6:00 A.M.

his mind, he knew what had happened to him and where he was. He was not shivering, but trembling with awe and expectation: But why was he alone? Where was Amy? The thought of her made him struggle to move his legs, to lift his head, and then to open his eyes.

What he saw was a world of white—around, before, beneath him. He raised his head higher to see better and pulled his legs up under him to get into a half-sitting, half-kneeling position. Blinking to free his eyes from snow and then adjust to the dazzle that all but blinded him, he saw a beauty he had not known before and to which his whole being made obeisance.

Far, far away was a distant line of hills like the ones his eyes had often rested on, so like but so unlike, for these were made of crystal and were shining as if they were translucent.

"The ramparts of heaven!" Bart breathed adoringly.

The sky beyond them was a blue so pale that it was almost no color, and as Bart gazed the mountains shimmered and glistened. Rivers of light began to emanate from them and flow down their slopes and across the white expanse that separated him from them. The rivers converged as they approached him, making a path for him to follow. Bart closed his eyes against the brilliance. When he opened them again, he saw that light was embracing him, that he was one with it.

"So this is it!" he said. "This is what it is like, white and shining. Everything clear, the near as well as the far. But where is Amy?"

He tried to stand so he might reach out his hand to take hers; then he told himself that it would not be her hand as in life but something more rare. It would be the warmth of her presence and his response: the way it had been so long ago when they had been drawn to each other.

Aware of the struggle that was going on within him as

Silver Lining

he yearned to find his way along the path of light, Bart saw his body as if it were a pile of old clothes he would soon be leaving behind. Pretty worn out, too, he thought, won't be much use even for a rummage sale at the church in Hemp-hill.

But why had he bothered to think of clothes when his being was filling with light?

"Amy!" he called. His voice had a hollow ring in the morning stillness.

The brilliance hurt, and he closed his eyes as pain stabbed them. He felt a twinge of pain in one leg, then in the other. He brought his mittened hands out of the snow and thumped them together; and pain shot through his fingers.

"No, oh, no," he moaned and sunk his head in his hands. It was then that he heard the barking of the dog. When Bart opened his eyes again, he shielded them from the light; he now knew what it was—the sun. Overflowing the world, it was reflected in a myriad of ways. The snow that had shrouded trees and bushes was commencing to fall away in great clumps and little clusters. As it fell it revealed ice-encrusted branches and twigs that gave the appearance of crystalline forms. Light playing on the crystal turned the trees into a company of jugglers tossing prisms into the air. It was short-lived; the ice was thin and the sun soon melted it. Where sound had been muffled, a pattering could be heard as moisture dropped from the trees pitting the smooth surface of the snow.

Bart moved his head, and snow shook away from the hood of his parka. He looked to the right, to the left, then to the line of hills ahead of him. They were his familiars, the limit of vision: they were not the ramparts he had thought them to be. He tried to move his body, but every move sent new waves of pain through him. Pain was a sign of life; that was the realization that shocked him into renewed

6:00 A.M.

struggle. How he had come to be lying in the snow or for how long were irrelevant matters; the snow was not the place for him to be and he was cold.

It was no longer the sound of Jock's barking but the feel of his warm tongue as the long nose pushed the snow aside and found familiar cheeks. Jock whimpered and pawed at the snow, digging it away in his attempt to get closer to the one he loved.

"Jock," Bart murmured, lifting his head, then dropping it again into the snow.

Now he heard voices beyond the tangle of branches from which he had fallen free.

Yes, there were people, Bart thought as his head began to clear. People, and one of them was a baby.

He endeavored to lift himself out of the snow, but the effort was not to be all his. Jock's paws had already made a clearing. Gabe and Val, knee-deep in snow, were on either side of Bart, getting their arms under him, lifting him, carrying him.

"Are you all right, Bart?"

"We'll get you to the porch, then we'll brush the snow off you. It's just a few steps."

"Yes, I'm all right." Bart found his voice as he found his way back to reality. "It was a soft fall." He tried to make his legs work for him, but even a few steps through deep snow were not soon accomplished.

"Where is everyone?" he asked.

Then they had reached the porch, and the two young men eased Bart down to sit on the step.

"We're here, Bart, we're all here, safe and sound."

Everyone started talking at once. What happened? How did he get in the snow? Wasn't it wonderful that Jock found him and dug him out? But what happened to him and was he all right?

Gabe and Val were busy brushing the snow off Bart,

feeling his arms and legs to make sure he had not been hurt in the fall. Bart found it hard to answer anyone. Then he saw the oak, the mesh of branches in the snow, the severed trunk.

85

"The house—is it all right?" he asked.

"Yes," Gabe said, "it was close, but you know the old saying—a miss is as good as a mile."

"The fall set up a tremor like an earthquake," Helen explained. "That and the crash woke us up, and we all came running out here to see what it was."

"A few bricks toppled off the chimney," Val added, "but there's no fire left in the stove now."

Bart was relieved. They were all right; the house was standing.

"But what happened to you?" They were asking him again. "How did you get out there in the snow?"

"Give me time, give me time." Bart tried to remember back to just what happened, and then he tried to find the words to tell them.

Waking from a doze and realizing how close the room was, he had gone up to the attic to open the window and let some air in. While at the window he had seen that a limb of the oak was swinging dangerously near the house. Bart put his hands up to his head. It had all happened so quickly it was hard to recall clearly just what he had done. He said as much as he could, as much as he would, then ended, with a slightly apologetic smile, "Well, here we all are."

Looking around at the group on the porch, Bart saw Zoe held in her mother's arms. She was cooing cheerfully to herself and playing with her fingers. Val, Gabe, and Helen were making the most of the sunlight that was flowing around them. The men had shed their coats and looked ready to start shoveling snow. There was no longer any silence: the patter made by snow melting from the roof and

6:00 A.M.

the thump as clumps of snow fell from the trees mingled with voices and laughter.

"I've never seen anything so beautiful," Helen said, and Val added, "So white, so dazzling white, and the sky so blue!"

Bart's return to reality enabled him to enjoy the scene, too. "It is a fine day, and we'll get ourselves dug out and down to the road in short order." He held his head sideways, listening. "Guess the plows are already at it."

Helen thought of her car, Gabe of his motorbike, but both were immobilized by more than snow.

Zoe's sounds began to change from delight in the morning to an inner need that made itself known in small plaintive cries.

"I expect that means she's hungry," Helen interpreted.

"You all must be." Bart, still the host, felt a responsibility toward his guests. He started to rise, then slipped back again.

"Wait, Bart, take it easy for a few more minutes. You had a mean fall, and the rest of us just got wakened up."

Against his will but yielding to their wishes, Bart sat back again. He loosened his parka, then took off his mittens. Thrusting one into each pocket, he found the two pieces of bread he had tucked in for the birds. He held them up offering them to Zoe.

"Look what I've found!"

Zoe squealed with excitement. Vera held her toward Bart, and she took a piece in each hand. Biting at the bread eagerly, she put first one piece into her mouth, then the other.

"That will keep her quiet for a while," Vera said. "Thanks, Bart. Now we can enjoy the morning a little longer."

Something wasn't right. Bart looked at the people sitting

Silver Lining

on, or leaning against, the porch railing. Someone was missing. "Where's Martin?"

They glanced around, almost expecting him to come through the door at the sound of his name. In the calamity of the tree, the need to rescue Bart, then the sheer bliss of sunshine and beauty of the white world, they had not thought of him.

"Must be the sound didn't wake him the way it did us," Val said.

The door to the house was half open. Helen, near it, peered in. "He isn't where I last saw him when I went to bed, in the chair by the stove."

"I'll go find him," Gabe said and went into the house.

From the woods nearby birds could be heard twittering, calling, as they flew and hopped about. From the road came the steady roar of plows. Day, with all its insistences, had taken over. Except for the oak and some small damage to the house, Bart surveyed the scene with a countryman's eye. There was no frost in the ground yet, so the snow would be absorbed in a few days. Water, always so needed before winter locked the land, would have a good depth. Wells would be full. Roots would be nourished. Jock pressed himself close to Bart, licking his face, his hands.

Bart laid a hand on the buff-colored head, then he fondled the dog's ears. There were some things of which he could be sure, and one of them was the feeling he and the dog had for each other. He patted Jock and murmured one of the pleasantries Jock understood.

Gabe stood in the doorway. "He isn't there."

The others stared at him.

Gabe looked dazed. "I mean"—he struggled for words—"he's there, but—"

"What do you mean, Gabe?" Val wanted answers, not riddles.

6:00 A.M.

Bart knew what he meant. "I'll help you, Gabe." He stood up. Now there was strength in his legs. He crossed the porch and went into the house joined by Val and followed by Gabe.

Helen and Vera looked at each other, each with a question that neither one voiced.

They found Martin at the base of the ladder where the bricks had scattered. One or more had caught at his head; though there was no open wound, there was a bruise that told its story. They carried him to the bedroom and laid him on the bed. Bart felt for any sign of life, a pulse in wrist or throat; he pressed his head close to the heart, but there was no beat, and the flesh was no longer warm.

He turned to the two standing beside him and shook his head.

"But—he seems to be smiling," Val said in a low tone.

Bart nodded. Had they not realized after an evening with the man what the smile meant, that it was as much a part of him as his hands, his hair.

"I—I've never seen death before," Gabe whispered. "I never knew it was—could be—beautiful."

Bart was unfolding the blanket that had been at the foot of the bed. Gabe and Val took hold of it, too, and they laid it gently, reverently, over the still figure. Then Bart put one hand on Gabe's shoulder, the other on Val's. The shock followed by the wonder in their faces touched him deeply. There was a wall that, apparently, neither one had yet come up to. Knowing it was there would do more than any words said, or to be said, to give life value.

"What shall we tell the others?"

"Tell them what has happened," Bart said simply, "that Martin has gone ahead."

Gabe and Val returned to the porch. Bart remained for a few moments with his friend. When he left the room, he closed the door behind him.

Silver Lining

They were talking in muted voices when Bart joined them, all except Zoe. She was playing with Jock in the snow, and her laughter rang out as cheerfully as the call of a chickadee. The sunshine was still as warm, the world still as beautiful, but they were subdued by the news that Gabe and Val had brought with them.

"He was our friend," Bart said, and the words were sufficient eulogy.

Bart sat down on the porch step and leaned back against a supporting pillar. The others sat on the railing or leaned against it as they had earlier. Each one knew there were things that must be done soon. Bart wanted to inspect the roof so repairs could be made to it and the chimney before another night came down. The young men were ready to clear a path down to the road. Helen and Vera felt that there might be some tidying to do in the house so it would be left in good order. But, for a time, no one wanted to do anything but think about Martin. He had touched their lives and given each one a new perspective. It would not be the only memorial service that would be held for Pastor Martin Amblin, but it would be the first.

They had been talking about Martin when Bart joined them, and they continued. From time to time Bart added an experience that he had had with Martin—and there were many—since his friendship with the pastor went back over the years. Others spoke of what he had meant to them during the hours of a stormy night, and the more they spoke the more easy and natural the tones of their voices became. Sometimes they found they could laugh at something remembered, something shared.

Bart, letting his eyes rest on one after another, thought how he had come to care for them during the time they were under his roof; on the edge of departure as they were, he realized he had come to love them.

Now they were talking not so much about Martin but of

6:00 A.M.

what lay ahead, the directions in which they would be going. They wondered if their paths would cross again, hoping that they would.

Gabe was the most forthright. With his head thrown back and the sunlight burnishing his golden curls, he spoke as if he had the shortest distance to go. "I have some business to do at the post office in Hemphill, then we shall see what we shall see."

"And that magnificent machine you call *Bucephalus*?" Val teased.

"It's up for sale."

Bart, watching Gabe, knew what he had known all along, that the golden curls were not real. Why did he do it? Bart wondered. Then he stilled his questioning as he often did by telling himself that it was no affair of his. If a man wanted to dye his hair, it was his hair after all, and he had a right to do with it what he chose.

Gabe turned to Bart. "I may be around here for quite a while."

Bart looked pleased. "My house is your home, and I can fix you up with a room if you need it. There's space in the shed once we get the chimney fixed."

"If we could meet your price, which we can't," Val began, "and if your machine would accommodate the three of us, which it can't, I'd buy it from you in a minute. It's not easy for a family to hitch it across the country."

"The 'ifs of history,' " Helen echoed an earlier conversation. Then she asked abruptly, "Where are you going?"

"To my folks," Vera answered. "They farm it in Kansas. It just might work out for us to stay with them for a while."

Val shook his head. "They'd feel better if we were married. That—that was something we were going to talk about with Martin this morning, but now—"

"Kansas!" Helen exclaimed, not in curiosity but amazement.

The two V's turned to her, startled first by the tone in her voice, then even more by her expression.

"Yes," Val said, "it's one of the fifty states, due west from here, known for its—"

Helen interrupted. "Don't give me a lecture on history, Val, just tell me how this can be. I'm on my way to Colorado and I go right through Kansas." She stopped short. She knew how this could be. "I've a big car and I'll be on my way as soon as the gas tank is filled. I'd be delighted to have you three with me. Perhaps you'll even share some of the driving."

A few hours ago when a child was being given a name, a smile had passed from one to another. It happened again. From Vera to Val, to Helen, to Gabe, to Bart the smile traveled, and back of it was the laughter of the child playing in the snow with a friendly dog.

Vera said, "I almost don't understand, and yet I think I do. Last night we didn't care what happened. Now we want to live, to go on." She slid off her perch on the railing and ran to Zoe. Picking her up in her arms, she hugged her as if she could never love her enough.

"What's that we're hearing?" Gabe cocked his head in the direction of the woods.

They all listened. It was Bart who interpreted the sound. "That'll be Ruel with his tractor, coming to dig us out."

Then it was as if they had said enough, and for the time that remained silence was needed: it was not memories that held their thoughts but plans. There was an underlying music in the sound of melting snow, the birds calling, the child prattling, the dog's sharp playful barks, the vibrato of plows on the distant road, the steady throb of the tractor making its way up through the woods. The sounds became a symphony, and those hearing it felt its exaltation. What might have been a requiem had become a *Te Deum*.

6:00 A.M.

"He'll be here soon," Bart said.

Helen went inside to collect her suitcase, Val and Vera to gather up their packframe and carrier. Gabe glanced down the road to where his motorbike stood, still shrouded in snow. All that he possessed or needed was in the sack buckled to the frame.

Bart, glancing through the open door, noticed the Swiss clock lying on the floor. He went to pick it up, pleased that it had not been broken in its fall, but it had stopped. He showed it to Zoe, who was sitting contentedly in a patch of sunshine on the porch.

"I've got something for you, young lady, and, if you'll let me, I'll fix it so you'll really like it."

He wound the clock while Zoe watched. Then he looked at the sky to confirm his sense of the time by the position of the sun. He set the clock at two minutes to nine. "That'll be near enough," he said as he held it up to his ear and smiled as the familiar ticking reassured him.

Zoe was charmed and made a clucking of joy as she reached toward the little clock.

Bart held it away from both of them. "In just a minute there'll be something for you to crow about."

Zoe took him at his word and waited, but her eyes never left the clock.

Silver Lining

9:00 A.M.

THE CLOCK tinkled the hour as tunefully as it had for all the years it had stood on the shelf in the Wilmers' house. Zoe listened, entranced. She clapped, then made a series of sounds in some kind of imitation. Reaching toward the clock, Bart put it in her hands.

"Oh, Bart—" Vera, returning to the porch, started to remonstrate.

"It's hers now," Bart said, "and it will keep time all the way to Kansas—and then some."

Val took Bart's hand. "You'll never know—" He couldn't finish what he wanted to say.

"I think I do know," Bart said, "I'm just glad that it was in my house, mine and Amy's house, that—" He could not finish what he wanted so much to say.

With a mercurial movement, Zoe thrust the clock at Bart and babbled demandingly.

"So! It's the chime you want to hear again! That won't be

until it comes around to ten o'clock, and there's nothing you or I can do to make it happen sooner."

She shook the clock in her insistence. Val took it from her and slipped it into the pocket of his shirt. Vera, cozying Zoe in her arms, forestalled an outburst of rage. Frustrated in her desire to hear the little clock's musical voice, Zoe's eyes blazed with fury and her lips turned tightly inward, but when Vera started to sway her back and forth a look of delight came over her face. Soon she was chortling gleefully, in time with the swaying.

"Perhaps she'll go to sleep again." Bart recalled the relief felt when one of his own, after what seemed ceaseless movement and endless chatter, had suddenly lapsed into quiet.

"Not likely," Vera replied, "but she'll be reasonable. She knows the clock is in her daddy's pocket."

Nearer and nearer came the sound of the tractor.

Ruel stopped on the edge of the woods, halted by the debris of the oak. The sound of the motor ceased. "Bart! Martin!" he shouted.

Bart went toward him through the snow in the track Gabe and Val had made when they pulled him out. "We need you." He breathed heavily as he grasped Ruel's hand. "I'm glad you came so soon."

Ruel stared at the tree.

Bart explained about the several people who had sought shelter during the storm, of the night spent under his roof, and then about Martin. "It was the bricks falling from the chimney."

Ruel, listening, reached up and took off his cap when Bart spoke of Martin. He held it in his hands in mute respect, then thrust it into a pocket. "I brought a pair of snowshoes up for him, but he won't need them now."

Bart shook his head. "But if you can somehow get the

Silver Lining

womenfolk into the cab, Ruel, the two men can go down on snowshoes, the pair you brought and mine."

"And you, Bart?"

"I'll wait here until you come back."

Ruel nodded. "It won't be long. Once I get the people and the child to my house, then you and I can take care of Martin." He looked at the mass of branches and limbs, at the shattered trunk, then shuddered. "A near miss to your house, Bart, but a good miss with all those people under your roof. I'm sorry about Martin, and I won't be the only one, but if he had to leave us I can't think of a better place than from your house." Looking at what was left of the oak, Ruel summed it up with a woodsman's eye. "You'll have cordwood for a year or more once we get this sawed and it seasons."

Bart nodded. "Two good friends in one night, Ruel. It's hard."

Ruel put his arms around Bart. Words had no meaning at such a time.

Together they trudged through the snow to the porch. Ruel quickly had the situation in hand, telling the two women to make their way to the tractor and get into the cab. "It'll be a tight squeeze but we'll manage, and once down at the house my wife has coffee and newly baked bread waiting for you." He smiled then as if to welcome them beforehand. "She thought I'd be coming back with just two. Now it's quite a crowd, but she's always got plenty." He tweaked Zoe's ears. "She'll like this one."

Bart took his snowshoes from the wall where they were hanging and handed them to Val. "I doubt that this web-footed walking is new to you."

Val slipped his feet into them and adjusted the harness with a practiced hand. "No, but I've never had such a good pair, nor ones in such good condition." He straightened

9:00 A.M.

up while Vera placed the carrier with Zoe riding in it over his shoulders.

Ruel brought the extra pair from the tractor and started to show Gabe how to adjust them. Gabe looked unbelieving as Ruel placed his feet where they belonged and tightened the straps. He wondered how he had once thought he could ever have made an escape on such contraptions.

"You mean I can walk with these things?"

"You'll feel free as a bird once you get going," Ruel said encouragingly.

"Free!" Gabe exclaimed. Then he said the word again, wanting to keep the taste of it on his tongue, in his mind.

"My car?"

"My motorbike?"

Ruel looked at Helen and Gabe. "As soon as the road gets open they'll be dug out and towed down to the garage. How soon do you need them?"

"As soon as possible, I've got a long way to go," Helen said. Then she amended the I to "We."

Gabe shrugged.

Bart stood on the porch and waved as they started toward the tractor. Ruel walked between the two women, giving a hand to each as they floundered through the snow. Zoe, riding on her father's shoulders, chirped like a bird at the new kind of locomotion provided by him on snowshoes. Gabe walked duck-footed at first; then, watching Val and his long strides, he soon caught on and moved easily over the snow. They all waved back to Bart, but Gabe was the only one who called out, "I'll be seeing you."

Voices were lost in the din of the motor. Then even its raucous sound diminished as it went off through the woods and down the incline to the Gibbses' house.

Bart sat on the top step of the porch. Jock pushed close beside him, responding with a lap of the tongue to the fondling of his ears.

"Amy," Bart said aloud—and then because he liked the sound and all that it meant he said it again—"Amy."

9:00 A.M.

CHRISTIAN HERALD ASSOCIATION AND ITS MINISTRIES

CHRISTIAN HERALD ASSOCIATION, founded in 1878, publishes The Christian Herald Magazine, one of the leading interdenominational religious monthlies in America. Through its wide circulation, it brings inspiring articles and the latest news of religious developments to many families. From the magazine's pages came the initiative for CHRISTIAN HERALD CHILDREN'S HOME and THE BOWERY MISSION, two individually supported not-for-profit corporations.

CHRISTIAN HERALD CHILDREN'S HOME, established in 1894, is the name for a unique and dynamic ministry to disadvantaged children, offering hope and opportunities which would not otherwise be available for reasons of poverty and neglect. The goal is to develop each child's potential and to demonstrate Christian compassion and understanding to children in need.

Mont Lawn is a permanent camp located in Bushkill, Pennsylvania. It is the focal point of a ministry which provides a healthful "vacation with a purpose" to children who without it would be confined to the streets of the city. Up to 1000 children between the ages of 7 and 11 come to Mont Lawn each year.

Christian Herald Children's Home maintains year-round contact with children by means of an *In-City Youth Ministry*. Central to its philosophy is the belief that only through sustained relationships and demonstrated concern can individual lives be truly enriched. Special emphasis is on individual guidance, spiritual and family counseling and tutoring. This follow-up ministry to inner-city children culminates for many in financial assistance toward higher education and career counseling.

THE BOWERY MISSION, located at 227 Bowery, New York City, has since 1879 been reaching out to the lost men on the Bowery, offering them what could be their last chance to rebuild their lives. Every man is fed, clothed and ministered to. Countless numbers have entered the 90-day residential rehabilitation program at the Bowery Mission. A concentrated ministry of counseling, medical care, nutrition therapy, Bible study and Gospel services awakens a man to spiritual renewal within himself.

These ministries are supported solely by the voluntary contributions of individuals and by legacies and bequests. Contributions are tax deductible. Checks should be made out either to CHRISTIAN HERALD CHILDREN'S HOME or to THE BOWERY MISSION.

Administrative Office: 40 Overlook Drive, Chappaqua, New York 10514
Telephone: (914) 769-9000